I0599180

Robert Davidson

Elijah

A Sacred Drama and other Poems

Robert Davidson

Elijah
A Sacred Drama and other Poems

ISBN/EAN: 9783337335236

Printed in Europe, USA, Canada, Australia, Japan

Cover: Foto ©Andreas Hilbeck / pixelio.de

More available books at **www.hansebooks.com**

Entered according to Act of Congress, in the year 1860, by

CHARLES SCRIBNER,

In the Clerk's Office of the District Court of the United States for the
Southern District of New York.

JOHN F. TROW,
PRINTER AND ELECTROTYPER,
50 Greene street.

REV. JOHN M. KREBS, D. D.

PERMIT me to inscribe this volume to you, as a mark, at once, of high personal regard, and a grateful recognition of your long-tried and constant friendship. As to the intrinsic merits of the work, you, who have not been without experience in this vein yourself, (can I forget " *Schlafen sie wohl ?* ") may be expected to be a lenient judge.

> " Hear then, attentive to my lay,
> For thou hast sung ! "

Should there be any grave personages ready to draw down their ominous eyebrows, as if the author were forsaking Mount Zion for Mount Carmel, or worse yet, for Mount Helicon, let them be informed, that the "Elijah" owed its origin to the seclusion of a sick-room; where, debarred for a season from active professional labor, the pen helped to beguile the tedium of a protracted confinement. It was under such circumstances, and propped up in bed by a mechanical contrivance, that the greater part of the poem was written.

As to the other pieces in the volume, it will suffice to say of many of them, that this is not their first appearance in print. The favor with which they have been received, and the fact of their having been copied into various periodicals, encourage the hope that it will not be deemed presumptuous if the waifs should now be collected together under one cover.

Meantime, let me call to your recollection, my friend, a sentence in one of Cowper's letters to Lady Hesketh, which, I hope, you will enjoy as much as I do. "I might," says he, "have preached more sermons than ever Tillotson did, and better, and the world would have been still fast asleep; but a volume of verse is a fiddle that puts the universe in motion." There is one small condition which Cowper omitted to mention, but which is quite indispensable to success; that is, provided you can get the universe, or even a respectable fraction of it, to listen to the music!

THE AUTHOR.

82 *West Eleventh street, New York,*
Sept. 17*th*, 1860.

CONTENTS.

———•••———

ELIJAH;

A SACRED DRAMA.

THE ARGUMENT.

ZEPHON, one of the Sons of the Prophets, to whom the caves of Mount Carmel afforded a refuge from the persecutions of Queen Jezebel, is joined upon the top of the mountain by Obadiah, King Ahab's pious steward, or more properly, major-domo, who narrates to him Elijah's challenge to the priests of Baal to meet him upon that spot for a solemn trial or ordeal by fire.

The procession enters. Chorus of Virgins of the Sun. The heralds announce the object of the convocation. While the altar is being constructed and other preparations made, the king proposes an argument between Elijah the prophet, and Amaziah, the priest of Baal, to which the latter reluctantly submits. Amaziah descants on the antiquity of the worship of the Sun, and its time-honored traditions. Elijah goes back to the birth of time and the creation of the sun by Jehovah. He alludes to its obeying the command of Joshua. He answers objections from the destruction of the Canaanitish nations. Hiel the Bethelite, an infidel, explains the myth of Adonis by the sun's return from winter to spring. Queen Jezebel interposes, extolling Sidon and other heathen capitals, for their improvement in taste, the arts, commerce, architecture, and the products of the loom, contrasted with the rudeness of the Hebrews. Elijah shows the superior value of truth and virtue. Maachah, the king's mother, upbraids the prophet with his severity. Ithobal, priest of the grove, the queen's chaplain, advises him to leave the vicinity of the court, and repair to the more congenial atmosphere of Judah. The prophet protests his willingness to endure martyrdom for his religion. The king abruptly closes the debate.

Chorus of priests of the Sun. In proportion as the day wears away without any answer by fire, their behavior grows frantic. Elijah taunts them with bitter irony. They become incensed, and Amaziah charges his presence as the obstacle to their success. He insists that the offended deity can be propitiated only by a human sacrifice, and demands the surrender of Elijah for the purpose. A great tumult ensues. Ahab protects him, and orders that the prophet offer sacrifice in his turn.

Elijah builds an altar, and drenches it with water. He prays. Fire descends from heaven, and consumes the sacrifice. The people, affected by the miracle, applaud, and vow their homage to Jehovah. Elijah orders the slaying of the priests of Baal at the river Kishon.

The poem concludes with a grand chorus of the sons of the prophets.

1*

THE PERSONS.

ELIJAH the Tishbite, the Hebrew prophet

ZEPHON, one of the sons of the prophets.

OBADIAH, King Ahab's steward, or governor of his house.

AHAB, king of Israel.

HIEL, the Bethelite.

AMAZIAH, priest of Baal or the Sun.

ITHOBAL, priest of the Grove.

MELZAR, chief astrologer.

ZADDIEL, a Hebrew.

HEZRON, a Hebrew.

MARSHAL and assistants.

JEZEBEL, queen of Israel.

MAACHAH, mother of Ahab.

CHORUS of priests of Baal or the Sun.

CHORUS of Virgins of the Sun.

CHORUS of the Sons of the Prophets.

HEBREWS, SIDONIANS, &c.

The *Scene* is the summit of Mount Carmel, looking to the sea. The *Time*, from morning till evening.

ELIJAH

ZEPHON, *alone.*

SOFTLY the sunrise stealeth o'er the sea,
The many-twinkling, many-sounding sea.
Its earliest kiss the snows of Hermon caught,
Suffused with virgin blushes; down it leaped
From peak to sparkling peak, with frolic haste,
O'er gloomy gorges and o'er rough ravines,
O'er dewy tamarisk slopes and broomy vales,
O'er pastoral plains, and dream-embosomed lakes,
Flooding with equal glory town and tower.
The shadow of the headland, that had stretched
Its giant bulk athwart the ample bay,
Shrinks back affrighted to the mountain's foot;
While o'er his level floor glad Ocean lays
A regal pathway, paved with flakes of gold.
Swift to the west the laughing Splendor flies,
To pash out the weak moon and pallid stars,
And strip the purple from discrownèd Night.
So spreads a smile from Childhood's happy lips,

Beams in the eye, and dimples in the cheek.
Till every feature shows the genial joy.

No cloud doth fleck the sky, nor ruffling breeze
Winnoweth wantonly the delicate spray.
The lazy shallops in the roadstead doze,
With blistered decks, and canvas idly furled.
The white-laced surf runs creaming up the beach,
Toying around the fisher's naked feet.
The solid sea, smooth to th' horizon's rim,
Seems a broad shield of gray and burnished steel,
Whereon Day's champion, rioting in strength,
His crest new-trimmed, ablaze with hornèd light,
Incessant flings a sheaf of golden darts,
Shivered as soon, and in a glittering shower
Resilient, as of topaz freshly broke.

Thou changeful, changeless Sea! all placid now,
As Infancy lulled by its cradle-hymn ;
But late we saw thy swirling billows huge,
Lush-green and foam-capt, madly chase along,
And bold the swimmer that would tempt thy spleen.
So sleeps the tiger, with retracted claw,
And sleek and shining skin.   A breath provokes,
Capricious termagant ! thy meekness feigned.
Thou battlest with the tempest at its top,
And hurl'st defiance to the thunder-cloud.
Down goes the bark that trusted to thy smile,
With all on board, strewing the ocean-floor

With ingots, jewels, silks of gorgeous Ind,
And costlier treasures earth were poor to buy.
Thou roll'st remorseless, heedless of the hopes
Thy frenzy wrecked. Perfidious, beauteous Sea!
We dote like lovers on thy fickle face,
Morn, noon, and fresh'ning eve, intent to spy,
But chief at glint of day, or rising moon,
New phases and aspects of loveliness.

The dreamy moan of thy perpetual surge,
Mysterious, plaintive, soul-subduing, low,
Intoning ever in the ear of Time,
Nature's entrancing chorus sweetly swells.
The Universal Hymn ascends ; none mute ;
Birds their shrill treble pipe ; the insect hum
Floats jocund on the liquid air ; winds blow
Their trumpet-blast, or sweep the forest-harp ;
Flowers swing their censers, steaming with perfume ;
The affluent accords still keeping time
Unto thy tidal pulses evermore ;
The bending skies drink in the solemn joy.
Thee, God ! the sea, Thee, earth and heaven praise.

OBADIAH *enters.*

OBADIAH.

Pardon my step abrupt, intruding thus
Upon thy early orisons : I come
Charged with grave tidings for the prophet's ear.

ZEPHON.

Welcome, thou faithful servant of the Lord,
Unspotted 'midst the vain, luxurious court,
My benefactor and protector thou!
Never forgotten is the dreadful day
When the queen's minions, all athirst for blood,
Against the prophets of the Lord went forth
To torture and to slay; thy generous care
At hazard of thine own the life preserved
Of full fourscore, concealed and fed within
The dusky covert of old Carmel's caves.
May He, who over sacrifice prefers
Sweet mercy, and provided in the law
For the birds' fledglings, well reward thy love!
But what contrives our subtle enemy,
Like the autumnal star, baleful as fair?

OBADIAH.

I will narrate in order, from the first.
As late I sought, amid the general drought,
Some tender meadow for the royal steeds,
Sudden the holy prophet, stern as wont,
In camlet coarse with leathern girdle bound,
Coming I know not whence, before me stood.
Awful he spake, the while, fear-paralyzed,
I sank upon my face: "Go, tell thy lord,
Elijah waits him here!" "Alas!" I cried,
"What is my fault, that thou shouldst work me harm?

Of every land the king exacteth oaths
They hold thee not, so covets he thy head.
Now thou art here, but soon a power unseen
Shall whirl thee hence, and when the king shall come,
Nor find thee, me deceiver will he brand,
And in the transports of his rage, will slay.
- Harm not, my lord Elijah! one from youth
God-fearing, to thy people ever kind."
" Distrust me not," he said, " thou art secure ;
Go tell the king, Elijah waits him here."
I sped my message.   Straightway rode the king,
And found the prophet in the selfsame spot.
" Troubler of Israel ! " he sharply spoke,
" What wouldst thou ? "   " Not to me belongs,"
Replied the man of God, " that keen reproach ;
'Tis thou and thine should wear it, having left
Jehovah's altar for a foreign god.
Hear now my challenge.   Bring to Carmel's top,
Before assembled Israel, Baal's priests,
And likewise all the prophets of the grove,
By hundreds reckoned.   There our several faiths
Put thou to trial, and be that avowed
The faith of Israel, which shall stand the test.
Who answereth by fire, let him be God."
" I marvel at thy boldness," said the king,
" Thou for an outlaw askest much, and great
The condescension that consents to this.
Be it as thou hast said ; but, mark me well,

Failure doth put in jeopardy thy head."
" So be it," said the seer, " equal the terms
To both.   Safe-conduct next I ask."
" For this occasion sole," replied the king.
They parted, and the royal mandate sped.

 The vast procession hither tends, and soon
Their barbarous music will fatigue thine ear.
With friendly haste I come my lord to warn
Of subtle secret plots against his life.
Not unobservant have I watched the arts
Of the queen's sleek and crafty chappellain,
Her favorite, the Sidonian Ithobal.

ZEPHON.

¹ Already see along the mountain side
The long procession upward winds its way.
First walk the oxen, marked for sacrifice,
With gilded horns, and streaming fillets decked ;
The sacred car, of ivory and gold,¹
With purple canopy, on pillars borne
Of silver, see ! by snow-white horses drawn,
Whose seat no mortal weight presumes to press.
But tell me, for the court thou knowest well,
Who are those women, beautiful but bold,
With open vestures given to the wind ?

OBADIAH.

The Virgins of the Sun thou dost perceive,²
Trained to the wanton dance and thrilling song.

In cloisters they the sacred wardrobe tend,
The richly broidered veils and priestly robes,
And, if belied not, skilled in softer arts.
Behind them throng the round and well-fed priests,
With thurible and sistrum.

ZEPHON.

     Who their chief?

OBADIAH.

'Tis Amaziah, from the lowest dregs
Upraised, like Jeroboam's vulgar priests ;
Of shallow learning, but with brow of brass.

ZEPHON.

What company is that, with sooty robes
And muffled heads, who seem to march apart ?

OBADIAH.

They the Chemarim are, and theirs the rites[3]
Due to th' Infernal Powers, whose baneful sway
They humbly deprecate with whine and howl.

ZEPHON.

And who are those with high and peakèd caps,
And wands all rough with quaint mysterious signs ?

OBADIAH.

The Casdim they, from far Euphrates' shore.
'Tis said they read the heavens as a scroll ;

They know the planets five, and the thrice ten
Celestial watchers, and the figured belt
Whose influences mark the natal hour.

ZEPHON.

Profane and blasphemous their occult trade!
The meek-eyed stars stoop not to watch our dust.

OBADIAH.

I marvel much why from the solemn pomp
The prophets of the grove, full twenty score,[4]
Are absent.   Can it be, the wily queen
Distrusts the issue of this challenge strange,
And means to screen her favorites from harm?
Or have they stood upon some jealous point
Of ceremonious precedency?

ZEPHON.

Explain why they her special favorites are.

OBADIAH.

Error is various; Truth is ever one;
So many sects, so many jealousies.
To Ashtaroth devoted is her zeal,
The Syrian goddess; in whose shaded groves[5]
What rites are held, beseems me not to say.
Samaria's temple-palace doth inclose[6]
A stately fane, where worshipped is the sun,
Adonis, Baal, Lord of light and heaven,

(Baal-zebub, the Fly-god, better named,)
Its cornices, its statues, censers, wrought
Of flaming gold.   In smaller chapels stand
The symbols of the Starry Host; and one,
To Heaven's queen sole dedicated, bears
No ornaments but silver.   Jezebel,
After Sidonian custom there resorts.
Black was the day that brought her to our shores,
With her outlandish and seductive ways!

ZEPHON.

Report doth give her charms beyond her sex.

OBADIAH.

Lithe as the willow, graceful as the palm
That waves by Elim's wells its plumy crown.
Nor is she shamed to snatch a grace from art,
With cunning pigments heightening her charms,
As roses swimming in a vase of milk.
Most gorgeous her attire, of Sidon's looms
The daintiest fabrics.   Foreign workmanship
Alone can answer her fastidious taste.
Not hers the modest and retiring grace
Which in the violet finds its lovely type,
Pure as the dew that fills its blushing cup,
Sweet as the scent exhaling back to heaven;
Chief ornament of woman, for whose loss,
Nor beauty makes amends, nor brilliant wit.

ZEPHON.

And what her disposition and her mind?

OBADIAH.

Beyond conception subtle and astute.
Such skill she hath in tongues, ambassadors,
Astonished, with interpreters dispense.
Her eye, its own expression taught to veil,
Looks down into the depths of other minds,
And reads their secret thoughts, its own unread.
She hath withal a soft persuasive voice,
That melts into the ear, and wins assent,
Without or proof or argument, to what she wills.
Fond of dissembling and intrigue, she bends
All things to her unscrupulous love of rule.
Winning her blandishments, but, when provoked,
No netted tigress more infuriate.
Secure she manages the easy king;
Give him his horses, and his Helbon wines,
And his Samarian harem, whoso will
May take the irksome toil of government.
In state she comes, surrounded by her guards,
As fits a queen.

ZEPHON.

                And hath she tricked our troops
In foreign armor, not the manly steel
Wherewith our valiant fathers glory gained?

Rounded their beards and hair, the which our law
Forbids.   Upon their stalwart breasts plate-mail
Of burnished silver flashes in the sun,
Their silver helms with disc and crescent topped.[7]
One hand supports a lance, the other wields
A circular targe of steel with gold inlaid.

OBADIAH.

Of foreign lineage are they ; none but such
The queen about her person tolerates.
Our Hebrews make not supple courtiers; stiff
Their necks and knees to ply the fawning trade.
But we must here arrest discourse, for see !
Th' impatient crowd are clambering up the steep,
Clinging to bush and crag, the shortest paths.
Soon will they stand upon the mountain's top.
Oh, vast assemblage ! oh, momentous day !
God of our fathers ! bare thy mighty arm,
The idol gods confound, and vindicate
Before the world thy worship and thy name !
Hence ! to the hoary prophet let us haste. [*Exeunt.*

(*Enter* MARSHAL *and* ASSISTANTS, *and* People.)

MARSHAL.

Quick, marshals ! to your posts.   The Circle trace,
Time-honored symbol of the Lord of Day.
The area clear.   Assign to each his room,
And keep the rabble close without the lines.

Set up the chair of state and canopy
On yonder knoll.   This mountain-height the air
Somewhat attempers.   On the sweltering plain
The heat and dust endurance do defy.
O for a shower, a cool, refreshing shower !

FIRST ASSISTANT.

Stand back ! stand back ! what, have ye no respect ?
Room for the king, I say !

SECOND ASSISTANT.

           By all the gods,
One might as well beat back the tide at flood.

MARSHAL.

Hark to the trumpets !   Each one to his place !

[*The Procession enters ; king* AHAB, *the queen,
their attendant trains, and a multitude of
people ; afterward* OBADIAH *and* ZEPHON.

ALL.

Long live the king !

SIDONIANS.

           And live queen Isabel ! [5]

AHAB.

At length the level summit we have gained   .
Of Carmel's well-poised mount, garden of God, [9]

And worthy of the name.   Its stony ribs
Health-breathing pines and lordly oaks adorn;
The hazy olives turn their linings up
Like silver lamps amid a night of green;
While copses of luxuriant laurel fringe
The rocky dells and sinuous ravines,
‑ Like a bride's tresses.   In profusion wild,
Anemone, that reddens in its cup,
In a fine tremble from the zephyr's kiss,
Crisp hyacinth, and modest asphodel,
Lend rarest fragrance to the loitering breeze.
And what a charming prospect courts the eye,
Of woods, and plains, and distant mountain-tops!
Lord-steward! as familiar with these scenes,
Describe the goodly landscape, point by point.

OBADIAH.

Truly familiar to me are these haunts;
For here in boyhood with my bow I roamed
To hunt the whirring partridge, or to trap
The stealthy fox that spoiled the early vines;
And from the crystal brooks oft slaked my thirst—
Yon crystal brooks that never cease their flow.
See distant Tabor looming up on high
A verdurous islet in the sere champaign.
There Sirion's range defines our northern bound,
Amana's peak, and Shenir wreathed in mist,
Where lions prowl, and leopards have their lair.

Outlined distinct against the glowing sky,
Lo ! Nature's priest, majestic Lebanon,[10]
In cope and mitre of unblemished snow,
Doth scatter dewy benedictions round.
His ancient cedars stand in rev'rent row,
The Levites of the sylvan sanctuary,
Their solemn psalm uplifting full and clear
To the responsive trumpets of the storm.
Southeastward see the long pale line that marks
The lordly pile near Jezreel newly built,
In wealth of myrtles, and of vines embowered,
With scarlet glories of pomegranates graced.
Commanding site, for princes fit retreat !

AHAB.

To round my park, an angle I require
Of the adjacent vineyard, but the churl
Denies the sale.   Whom all the gods confound !

JEZEBEL.

Thou shalt, my lord, possess it ; rest at ease.
A king should find his lightest wishes law,
Else were the golden round a barren toy.

OBADIAH.

Beneath us undulates the battle-plain
Of Esdraelon ; as our fathers tell,
There Barak, like a torrent, from the height
Of Tabor, rushed impetuous.   Not the strength

Of iron chariots could resist the stroke.
The sword devoured its thousands, drunk with blood,
And ancient Kishon swept them to the sea,
Yon westering sea, where Carmel dips his foot.
The blue expanse melts in the bluer sky
Flecked with the fleets of Tarshish and of Tyre,
The land of Caphtor, and far Chittim's isles.

JEZEBEL.

Oh, blessed, blessed sea! that laves the shores
Of my beloved Sidon. When shall I,
My country! see thy tide-kissed walls again,
Thy piers, thy palaces, thy princely pomp?

ITHOBAL.

Madam, restrain thy tears, I do implore:
The nobles see this passionate burst ill-pleased.

JEZEBEL.

Excuse, my lords, my feelings' ardent gush!
The tears would flow at sight of the blue waves
That wash my old, beloved, ancestral halls.
The shell will murmur of its ocean-home;
The prisoned dove its native wood-notes trill;
The smitten flint its heart of fire betray.
Nature hath had her due, and I am calm.

2

AHAB.

Heralds! make proclamation of the cause
That here convenes us.

HERALD.

Be it known to all,
Our sovereign lord the king, of his good pleasure,
Doth convocate the tribes upon these heights,
That solemn ordeal may be made betwixt
The two religions, Baal's and Jehovah's.
Three years of drought have turned the earth to iron,
The heavens to brass. The herbage is burnt up.
The husbandman distraught, doth thrust his knife
Into the veins of his last ox, to quench his thirst.
That altar, whereupon the fire from heaven
Shall swift descend, and burn the sacrifice,
To be succeeded by refreshing showers
Of copious rain, shall instant be confessed
The altar of the True and Only God. There bow
The grateful nation, and no other own!
With this condition; whichsoever party
Shall fail, do put in jeopardy their lives
A forfeit and atonement to the God.

AHAB.

Call the Chartummim and Astrologers.
Melzar, are all the auguries auspicious?

MELZAR.

May the king live forever! by the rules
Of divination, freely pecking birds,
The bright sons of the quiver duly drawn,
Chaldean numbers big with coming fate,[11]
The aspects and conjunctions of the stars,
There never shone a more auspicious hour.
Fearless proceed the issue must be happy.

MAACHAH.

But where's the vaunting prophet, at whose call
Kings, priests, and commons crowd these flinty
    heights?
Or does he mock us? for, in sooth, no law
His savage nature owns but his caprice.

HIEL.

Mayhap the holy man hath of his fears
Taken wise counsel, dreading a defeat;
For blusterers, when subjected to the test,
Oft, like a treacherous bow, do swerve aside.
Trust me, my lord, he'll hardly show his face,
Or here obtrude his sanctimonious cant.

AHAB

What saith my steward? for thou first didst bear
His message.   Wilt thou now the surety be
For his appearance?

OBADIAH.

My most gracious lord,
Misdoubt him not; within that rind austere
Lie rugged honesty and downright truth.
Averse to rites of worship he loves not,
He but delays till they have been performed.
I'll answer for his presence with my life.

JEZEBEL.

I would your Grace would put him under ban,
And set a price upon his stubborn head.

AHAB.

My queen, what have we now to apprehend
From a defenceless and unarmèd wretch,
Whose followers have melted all away
Like snow in Salmon? Not a tongue is found
To lisp against our fair establishment.
The fang's extracted.

JEZEBEL.

But the venom's left.

AHAB.

Whence is thine unrelenting enmity?

JEZEBEL.

The presence of reprovers is unwelcome,
Though from their lips no syllable escape.

Rude as his shaggy garb his manners are,
As blunt to queens as to their tiring-maids.

AHAB.

I too dislike him, yet I feel there's good
'Neath that rough outside. Would he were my friend!
- Marshal! the ceremonies may proceed.

[*An altar is erected. The Virgins of the Sun
chant the Hymn of Inauguration. At the
close of every strophe, they dance round the
altar in a circle.*

Chorus of the Virgins of the Sun.

I.

Beat the ground with briskest measure,
Bound each pulse with liveliest pleasure!
Merrily the sistrums tinkle,
Rapidly the white feet twinkle;
Round and round in mystic ring,
Choir of planets symbolling! [13]
Joy and rapture rush along
On the swelling tide of song;
And with warm exultant strain,
Greet the Day-god's welcome reign!

II.

Hail th' auspicious moment, hail!
Over hill and over dale,

O'er the rivers, o'er the sea,
Streams the dazzling majesty.
First the courier of the dawn [13]
Wakes the lark upon the lawn,
Till from every feathered throat
Richest symphonies upfloat;
And with warm exultant strain,
Greet the Day-god's welcome reign!

III.

Nor alone the birds and flowers
Gratulate the rosy hours;
Busy hands and earnest hearts
Rouse to act their wonted parts;
Toils of peasants, cares of kings,
Traffic with its woven wings;
All the joyous world's astir,
Leaping from night's sepulchre;
And with warm exultant strain,
Greet the Day-god's welcome reign.

IV.

Weary lid and fevered head,
Tossing on a sleepless bed;
Mothers, half with terror wild,
Bending o'er a moaning child;
Sentries pacing at their post;
Sailors off a dangerous coast;

Frequent turn a longing eye
To the flushing eastern sky;
And with warm exultant strain,
Greet the Day-god's welcome reign.

V.

By the laughing Hours attended,
Onward moves the pageant splendid;
Dappled Dawn with diamond dew,
Sunset pomp of Tyrian hue; ·
Spring, with green and tender shoots,
Autumn, with its luscious fruits;
Men, who thrive these gifts upon,
Pour their grateful benison;
And with warm, exultant strain,
Greet the Day-god's welcome reign.

ELIJAH *enters, with the Sons of the Prophets.*

AHAB.

In a good hour thou comest, hoary seer!
To save thy name from damage, and thy truth;
Already had the whisper gone abroad,
That thou thy cause had yielded by default.

ELIJAH.

My liege! I come to pay the homage due
The ruler of my country, faithless else

To my religion and the holy Law,
Which curse disloyalty.   Not mine the tongue
To sow sedition, or disturb the realm.
The sword and sceptre are from God; by him
Kings reign, and princes judge with equity,
And likest him they show, when found most just.
For magistracy is of God ordained
A social blessing, anarchy and crime
To banish, and the feeble to defend.
Raised to the topmost round of power, for this
They to the King of kings shall give account.
No traitor I, no dark conspirator.
Were I admitted to thy counsels, prince!
Thy throne should stand upon a firmer base,
And thou shouldst be a king indeed, uncurbed
By priestly malisons and auguries,
That hidden power, o'ershadowing the throne.

AHAB.

By Tammuz' wounds, I like thy frankness much;
Such speech hath long been strange unto mine ear.
Thou shalt my prophet be, my chapellain,
Director of the royal conscience, not
An idle sinecure.   But to the point:
The tribes are met, the solemn ordeal waits;
Dost thou not shrink, thy single self opposed
To overawing numbers?

ELIJAH.

Not alone
Stands the brave champion of a holy cause;
Greater and more his friends are than his foes
Fire-chariots of the sky encompass him;
The angels count his every step; the just
And good bend from their heavenly thrones to give
Their approbation and their sympathy.
And should he fall, his infinite reward
Dies not. The listening ages catch his name,
And send it onward. Like a trumpet's blast,
Men's hearts do leap within them at the sound;
Heroic virtue gains new suffrages,
And from the martyr's ashes spring fresh fires.
Why should I quail? To God I trust my cause;
Who feareth God can have no meaner fear.[15]

AHAB.

Ho! Amaziah! 'twere a pleasant thought,
Now that confronted are the chiefest men
Of these adverse religions, that ye hold,
The whilst the sacrifices are prepared,
An argument to entertain the time.

AMAZIAH.

My lord, O king! 'twould be a compromise
Of dignity, for us to condescend

2*

To argue with schismatics.   Only that
Which owns its likely fallibility
Seeks and rejoices in debate, as if
In noise and clamor weakness to conceal.
But our religion needs no argument;
It on prescription, not on reason, stands.
Ours is the old religion, handed down
From hoar antiquity.   And who but knows
That from the earliest times, while Moses was
A slave in Egypt, nor yet had despoiled
The Emims and Zamzummims of their lands,
The king Adonis, lord of Light and Day,
Received the homage of the Syrian maids.
Before his orient pomp the prostrate world,
As now, with early reverence, adored.
Ev'n Abraham, their vaunted patriarch,
A Chaldean was, and worshipper of fire.

ELIJAH.

What though a thousand years have come and gone,
Since, from the second cradle of our race,
'Twixt Ararat's twin peaks, the nations swarmed,
And all that time in error's chains were bound?
What though our ancestors, ere Abram's day,
In Aramæa, blind idolaters,
Bowed to the Sun or Fire?   No lapse of time
Can Error's nature change, or consecrate.
Error is Error still, nor can be Truth,

Though one be but the outbirth of an hour,
The other claim the centuries for its own.
Talk we of hoar antiquity ?   Lead back
Thy thoughts to that majestic hour, when first
God into being spake the Earth and Heaven.
Over the vast Eternal Silences
In Night and Horror veiled, rang forth the word,
" Let there be Light ! " and from the chaos, Light
Sprang forth obedient, all the infant worlds
Revealing ; while the glorious Sons of God,
Bright morning-stars, in chorus sang for joy.
Then first the sun, a new-made orb, was set
To rule the day, the moon to rule the night,
In peaceful and unwearied ministry,
Jehovah's will fulfilling, for man's good.
And short the homage stops, that stays on them,
Mere servants without mind or life, nor higher
Rises to the great Hand that lit their fires,
To creatures giving the Creator's due.
What courtier suing to his gracious king,
Lavishes on the scribe his bursting thanks,
And for the royal donor has no praise ?

AMAZIAH.

Blank atheism !   What ! the glorious Sun
Nought but a globe of fire, a vulgar lamp,
For meanest deeds of meanest men devised !
Sublimer views are ours ; that gorgeous orb,

Upon whose blinding splendors none may gaze,
The palace is of Sovereign Deity,
His seat and dwelling-place, his flaming throne,
Majestic chariot, whence he guides the spheres.
Not otherwise the Moon, and several Stars,
Showering down radiance from their golden urns,
Are the abodes of gods, of spirits bright,
Presiding o'er the elements, man's natal hour,
The growth of empires, or their threatened fall.

ELIJAH.

Not me, rather thyself an atheist deem,
Who dost the true and only God deny.
Which of thine idols, wood, or brass, or stone,
Silver or gold, hath made and fashioned thee
And giv'n thee breath?   How could they aught
    create,
Themselves the fragile work of human hands,
Half on a shrine, and half behind the hearth?
My God Creator is of Earth and Heaven,
And all things in them that do live or move.
Where were these mighty gods, these sovereign
    powers,
With high celestial influences impregned,
When the five kings before great Joshua fled?
" Sun, stand thou still on Gibeon ! " he cried,
" And stay, thou Moon, o'er Ajalon's deep vale ! "
They heard the mandate, and their fervid wheels

Arrested in mid-heaven ; nor e'er was known
A day so long as that, when at the voice
Of mortal man the heavens obedient stood
To help him rout their faithful worshippers.
Strange ! they should listen rather to their foe,
Deaf to their votaries' despairing prayer !
- These are thy gods, Samaria ! put to shame
Before Jehovah, true and only God,
The God of Gods, the Lord of Hosts, Most High.

Amaziah.

And canst thou glory in a cruel God,
Ruthless and partial, giving to the sword
Whole unoffending nations, whose sole fault
Was fighting for their altars and their homes
Against the insults of a foreign horde ?
The patriot's meed, the patriot's wreath, be theirs !

Elijah.

In holy horror to lift up thine hands
At thought of cruelty, doth well become
Those who to devils sacrifice their sons,
To Canaan's idol-gods their daughters dear !
Now hearken, and thy calumny retract.
From Egypt fled, asylum Israel sought,
Molesting no one on their peaceful way,
Till first themselves assailed by every king
From Zoar unto Zidon, passage free

Refusing, or opposing them in arms.
Compelled to self-defence, they drew the sword,
Putting their foes to ignominious rout;
And thus they won themselves a resting-place.
Claim not the patriot's hallowed name or meed
For wretches stained with deeds of lust and blood,
Who tossed their smiling babes to Moloch's fires.
The land, unable longer to sustain
Their vile abominations, spued them forth;
A holy God beheld their measure full.
His high prerogative it is, to use
Famine or earthquake, pestilence or sword,
To sweep profane transgressors from the earth.
Behold the Vale of Siddim scathed with fire,
And sunk beneath the sullen Sea of Salt,
Whose ruined cities, smothered in their lust,
Attest the justice of avenging heaven.

   And these abominations ye would fain
Lift to the shrine once more, your dunghill gods
Seeking to please with rites detestable.
Repent! and to the bats your idols fling,
Or robed in vengeance shall the Lord unlock
The armory of heaven.   Then shall his eye
Spare not nor pity.   Think not it shall prove
A mountain-echo vain.   On foreign shores
Exiled and naked, labor-sore and sad,
The heathen whom you copy, shall you serve;
Already buds the rod of chastisement,

The web is wove that mantles you with shame.
Oh Israel! oh my country! shun the fate
Which heaven-daring wickedness insures;
O Israel, hear! The Lord thy God is ONE!

ZABDIEL, (*aside.*)

- His words do stir me like a trumpet's sound,
Waking up long-forgotten memories;
I learned them, standing by my mother's knee,
A happy child of innocence and prayer.

HEZRON, (*aside.*)

It is too true; the land in mourning lies
For crimes at which humanity may weep,
While Modesty conceals her blushing face.
Like priest, like people! Princes and the crowd
Follow with greed these base enormities.

HIEL THE BETHELITE.

Why quote the legends that have had their day,
Long antiquated and exploded quite!
The world is wiser grown, and in these myths
Of Tammuz, or Osiris, or Adonis,
Of Isis or Astarte, we discern
Profoundest truths of astronomic lore,[17]
Seasons and solstices prefiguring.
'Tis a fair thought with dance and song to hail
Nature reviving from her wintry trance,

And from her icy fetters joyful freed;
Spring, with its buds and birds, and breath of balm,
Its blowing flowers, and opulence of leaves;
A resurrection from the shades of Death.
   But for those Hebrew writings, none that prize
A name for culture or a liberal mind
Respect their superstitious legends weak
Of worlds made out of nothing, when we know
Matter must be eternal; and of gods
That plagued th' Egyptians in the wilderness.
'Tis the same books denounce a curse on him [18]
Who would the City of Palm-trees dare rebuild.
The curse has harmless stood and will; and I
.Am he who will expose it to contempt.

ELIJAH.

Behold! the messenger is on his way
To tell thee the foundation hath been laid
Now in thy first-born's blood. One after one
Shall of thy children follow, giving space
For thought and for repentance, which if thou
Fail to improve aright, the lofty gates
Shall in thy youngest darling be set up.

JEZEBEL.

'Tis not for me to enter in the lists
Of keen polemics. Theologic war
Suits nor my sex nor taste. Not judgment cold,

But warm instinctive impulse governs me.
Much more congenial to my woman's heart,
Than a stern God, in storm and thunder drest,
Is she who glides, a gentle patroness,
In silver shallop 'mid the island-stars,
The mild Astarte, to our frailties kind,
Full of a mother's sympathy for all.
Sweet mother! Queen of Heaven! be hers my vows,
The incense, and the monthly offering!
But harsh thy creed, old man! and rude thy speech,
Rough as the sea, when boisterous Cadim blows,
Or winds Etesian chafe the billowy waste.
Unpolished and uncouth thy native tribes,
Beside the more refined and courtly realms
Of wise old Egypt, or Assyria grand,
Sidon, the populous mart of all the world,[19]
Or Tyre, her island-daughter, young and fair.
There taste is nursed, there elegance presides;
There art and science all their marvels show;
There commerce dazzles with her wealth of wares,
Exquisite products of the wheel and loom,
Spices, and gems, and royallest of dyes;
The very sands with crystal treasures teem.[20]
Shrines, temples, stately palaces adorn
Each avenue, and charm the stranger's eye.
A thousand keels, dripping with foreign brine,
Borne down with rich freights to the water's edge,
The harbor throng, luxuriously equipped

With broidered sails and banks of ivory.
    How far beyond the base simplicity
Of the half-tutored Hebrews, who can show
No arts, no commerce, no soul-breathing forms
By master-hands from purest marble wrought!
Nay, when the only temple that they boast
Was at vast cost of toil and treasure reared,
Unequal to the task they stood confest.
Sidonian builders shaped the mighty pile,
Sidonian skill the cedars carved, and hewed
Column and cornice from the stubborn stone.
Say, which the better creed, most worthy heaven,
Which most embellishes and brightens life?

ELIJAH.

What are the vaunted miracles of art,
The sumptuous colonnade, the sculptured pomp,
The thrift of trade, the niceties of taste,
The sophist's swelling words, the harp's sweet tones,
What to the welfare of a deathless soul!
A soul in ruins! an immortal mind,
By error led astray, and kindred vice,
Fall'n like a star from heaven; its glory-robes
Besmirched and sullied in the mire of sin!
Better to starve in honest rags, than roll ·
A pampered wanton, to the shades of death;
Better the uncouth peasant, rude in speech,
Who knows the true God and him knowing loves,

Than the proud prince who bows to idols false,
And as he bows, proclaims his deeper shame.
With pen of iron and point of diamond writ,
The Truth of God defies the tooth of Time,
Imperishable 'mid the world's wild wreck,
When Noph and Nineveh shall buried be.

    And thou, gay, godless Sidon, drunk with wealth,
Thy revenue the harvest of the sea ;
Thou that the people of the Lord dost scorn,
And tempt them with thy vile idolatries ;
The sword without, and pestilence within,
Shall lay thy princes low ; the captive yoke
Shall gall thy neck ; deserted and decayed,
Thy silt-choked harbor and thy beggared site
Shall to the far-off ages loud proclaim,
Who God dishonor, shall dishonored be.
Howl, haughty Tyre ! thy glory taketh wing ;
Prepare the sackcloth and the ashes strew !
I hear the shout of war, the clashing lance,
The trampling hoof, the hollow-rumbling wheel,
The tower and rampart thund'ring to the dust,
And leaving thee a bald and naked rock.
Ye nations, pass the cup of trembling round,
Nor dare to put it from your vice-worn lips !

MAACHAH.

Old man ! thou art severe ; thou hast no ruth,[21]
No pity in thy soul.   Thy veins were filled
Not from a woman's, but a tiger's breasts.

ELIJAH.

Not so! God knoweth, who shall be my judge,
'Tis not from native love of savageness,
Nor from delight in pain, that I employ
Warnings and threatenings to deter from sin.
Not to my sympathy in vain appealed
The widow of Sidonian Zarephath,
Nor none o'er her reviving son more joyed.
Unfeeling call me not! My heart doth bleed
To see my people perish for the want
Of thought, like ships upon the breakers driv'n.
Most willingly, t' avert th' impending fate,
On mine own head I'd call the thunders down.
Sole witness for the true religion left,
With bitter tears and groans I cry aloud,
O Israel, hear! The Lord thy God is ONE!
'Tis thou, O queen! that playest the cruel part,
For thou thy rightful influence dost abuse,
To lure thy son to worship Baalim,
Their ruin thus assuring, and his own.

ITHOBAL.

Prophet, forbear! thou touchest delicate ground;
The sanctity which princes doth environ
Should be preserved inviolate. If thou
Must prophesy of ill, to Judah turn,[22]
Where with congenial bigots thou may'st herd;

But vent not thy rebukes where courtly ears,
Fastidious, are to smoother language used.

ELIJAH.

Truth is the passion of my soul.   For Truth
I'd tread the burning marl, or dare the rage
- Of lions and of leopards, or of men
  More fierce than either.   Unappalled I'd stand
Beneath the frown of power, or face the shock
Of the incensed and surging multitude,
By prejudice and malice hounded on.
Torn be my tortured body limb from limb,
My martyr heart hiss in the curling flames,
Ere I the word of God should compromise!
Soon as the Spirit Divine, with hallowed fire,
Exalting sense and soul, my lips doth touch,
All meaner objects vanish from my sight,
Nor thrones nor dungeons dazzle or confound.
The word put in my mouth I'll speak, if men
Lend or refuse their ears.   Be it that ye wish
No further parley!   Let us to the test.
Less than a miracle will not suffice
This contest to decide.   Who answereth
By fire, O Israel! he shall be thy God.

AHAB.

A limping course hath this debate pursued,
Like every other, leaving either side

Just where it found them.   As for my dull brain,
Stunned by these subtleties, sufficeth it
I am th' anointed ruler of this realm.
'Tis my prerogative to legislate
In civil and ecclesiastic things supreme.
With rights of conscience I ne'er interfere,[23]
All as they please may think, but must conform
To the established worship.   Odious schism
And factious discord I abominate,
Nor license disobedience to the laws.
Go, heralds! bid the holy priests prepare
The gravest rites of their religion now,
And in our dire distresses spare no pains
To make the immortal gods propitious to us.

ELIJAH.

Aye, bid them spare no pains, put forth their strength,
And summon all th' array of their resources.
How long 'twixt two opinions will ye halt,
O Israel! as cripples sway about,
Or as a bird that hops from spray to spray,
And settles upon neither?   If convinced
Jehovah is the true and only God,
Almighty, all-sufficient, perfect, good,
Give him your homage, pay to him your vows.
If Baal be the true and living God,
Serve Baal; for ye cannot worship both.
Why silent all? and have ye ne'er a word

To answer me, from policy or fear?
Why, see! I, only I, one feeble man,
Am left of all the prophets of the Lord,
While twenty score are ranged on Baal's side;
What have ye then to fear with such vast odds?
Give us two bullocks; and let Baal's priests
Make their selection, dress their sacrifice,
And lay it on the altar; but no fire
Put 'neath the wood, as is their wont to do.
I will the other bullock treat likewise.
Then call ye on your gods; and I will call
Upon the sole name of Jehovah-God.
And let the God who answereth by fire
Be publicly confessed the only God.
Must not the God of Fire his votaries hear?
Is not the element at his command?
Shall it be said, he either lacks the power,
Or else the will, to send the kindling flame?
And lacking either, does he merit homage?
Are ye content?

ALL.

We are; thou hast well said.

HERALD.

The altar's reared, the sacrifice disposed,
They wait but for the royal word.

AHAB.

Proceed.

[*The Priests of Baal march round the altar,
singing in chorus, and dancing vehemently at
the close of each strophe.*

Chorus of the Priests of Baal.

I.

Dread Lord of heaven, sole source of day,[21]
To whom our constant orisons we pay,
Hear us, great king !
Adoni, hear !
Thee we revere,
Accept our offering.

II.

Behold our blighted fields !
No fruit the olive yields,
No more the land with milk and honey flows ;
The pools and fountains fail,
The fainting cattle wail,
Bashan is parched, and faded Sharon's rose.
O vine of Sibmah, mourn !
Upon the car is borne
No more the shout of merry vintagers ;

The presses all are still ;
On valley and on hill
No voice of joy the slumbering echo stirs.

III.

Beautiful Water : best gift of the sky,
Cool to the touch, and clear to the eye ;
Hidden deep in the shaded well,
Bubbling up from the mossy dell.

Beautiful in the rocky grot,
Where the heats of noontide enter not ;
In the dewy pearls that sprinkle the lea,
In the shimmering lake, and the dimpling sea.

Beautiful in the rainbow bright,
Woven of mists and threads of light ;
Beautiful in the vernal shower,
Greening the leaf, and tinting the flower.

Beautiful in the sandy waste,
The Eye of the Desert, with palm trees graced ;
With frantic joy the caravans cry,
Beautiful Water ! best gift of the sky.

Windows of heaven, open again,
Refresh once more the thirsty plain !
Merciful Lord ! thy suppliants spare,
Close not thine ear to a nation's prayer !
3

IV.

Why do thy quenchless ardors burn,
Why dost thou our petitions spurn,
Why do thy fire-tipt arrows fly
Vengeful athwart the brazen sky?
Thy altars we have not forsaken;
The holy fire
We have not suffered to expire;
And freely hath the choicest of the herd been taken.

V.

Not thus did Nature mourn,
Dishevelled and forlorn,
When, in the shady Syrian grove,
The queen of Beauty and of Love,
Her divine and perfect charms
Gave to thy consenting arms.
All nature breathed of happiness;
From their gold-lipped chalices
A thousand flowers sweet odors shed
To grace thy happy nuptial-bed.
All the dreamy noon was still,
Save the rippling of the rill,
And the doves, with breasts of snow
Cooing soothingly and low;
Slumberous zephyrs softly sighed,
Kissing myrtles soft replied;

Sifted through the leafy screen,
Mellow light fell, golden-green ;
All thy faculties entrancing,
Every pulse with rapture dancing ;
Thus, in the shady Syrian grove,
The hours were given to thee and love.

VI.

By those thrilling ecstasies,
By that lunacy of bliss ;
By their fond remembrance now,
Clothe with smiles once more thy brow ;
  Hear us imploring,
  See us adoring !

VII.

Recall that day of woe,
When to the chase thou fain wouldst go ;
In vain thy queen around thee clung,
In vain prophetic warnings filled her tongue.
Then met thee, in the forest lone,
The cruel boar of Lebanon :
See his visage grim and dusk,
His bloodshot eye, his horrid tusk !
The slender spear within thine hand
Could not his powerful charge withstand ;
Rushing like a wintry storm,
He dashed to earth thy lissom form ;
And ripping up thy naked side,
Tore a ghastly wound and wide.

So a lily, frail and fair,
Cloven by the ruthless share,
Sudden droops its beauteous head,
Sinking on the turfy bed.

VIII.

From that wound thy life's warm blood
Welled amain in stanchless flood,
Dabbling all thy sunny hair;
Thy body, delicate and fair,
Smooth as rosebud of the spring,
In clotted gore enveloping.
It bathed the wind-flower growing nigh,
And tinged it with a sanguine dye;
Then, trickling onward to the river,
Incarnadined its waves forever,
And flower and river still retain
The memory of that mournful stain.[25]

IX.

What words the frantic grief can paint
That poor Astarte's bosom rent,
As by that mangled corse she sate,
Utterly disconsolate!
The Syrian maids, with sobs and sighs,
Mingled their deepest sympathies,
Seated like mourners on the ground:
  "Tammuz is dead!" the woods,[26]
  "Tammuz is dead!" the floods,
"Tammuz is dead!" the rocky hills rebound.

X.

Upstarting from her trance of grief,
From heaven the goddess seeks relief,
And all her potent influence wields;
Reluctant Death his victim yields.
   Tammuz revives,
   He lives, he lives!
Restored to upper air,
Again the joys of life and love to share.
   The Syrian maids
   Bid woods and glades
Once more re-echo his beloved name.
And Nile from Byblos learns to celebrate his fame.

XI.

And still, from year to year,
With songs and dances they appear;
And still, from age to age,
All people in thy praise engage;
Whether with flowing hair and foot of gold,
Thou dost the portals of the Dawn unfold,
Or sett'st 'mid gorgeous piles of crimson glory,
All climes and tongues rehearse the pleasing story.
   Then hear our prayer!
   Lowly we bend,
   Deliverance send,
   Sweet Tammuz, hear!

XII.

God of day,
    Prince of light,
Disperser of clouds,
    Scatterer of night;
Adoni great,
    Sphered in splendor,
Life of the world,
    Our health's defender,
Hear, Baal, hear,
Answer our prayer!

ZABDIEL.

If in vociferation prayer consist,
Or clamor be the test of piety,
Then iron lungs and throats of brass must rate
The chief equipment of superior saints.
Prayer is the quiet breathing of the heart,
The lowly whisper, or the contrite sigh,
Which He who made the heart interprets well;
Only when calm, the lake reflecteth heaven.
See how they toil and sweat, at vast expense
Of nerve and muscle, vaulting in the air,
While " Baal! Baal! Baal! " is their cry,[27]
Repeated o'er and o'er, a thousand times.

HEZRON.

And see, as with a sudden frenzy seized,
They leap upon the altar, and with shouts

And mad contortions, cut with lancets keen [28]
And sacrificial knives, their arms and breasts.

ELIJAH.

Loud and yet louder lift your urgent voice,
And spill the crimson tide, whose stream delights,
Sweeter than incense, your blood-thirsty god !
Louder and louder cry ! spare not your breath !
For sprung from mortals, to your god may cleave
Some weaknesses of frail mortality.
Perchance he sleeps ; for now 'tis past high noon,[29]
When gods do oft retire to cover up
Their feet, and slumber in some cool recess.
Perchance he tarries in the nether world,
Not having heard the vivifying voice
That terminates his hybernation drear.
Perchance with Ashtaroth he converse holds,
And as he lips his leman, fails to catch
Your feeble supplications. Or, mayhap,
Fond of the chase, again he flies the boar,
And drops again beneath the deadly tusk.
Or, it may be, on Ethiopian hills,
A twelve days' journey gone, he keeps a feast,
And nectar sips 'mid all his jocund troop,
Nor heeds the miseries of mortal men.
Cry, cry aloud ! Shout till your throats are hoarse,
For day is waning, and as yet no voice
Nor answering sign gives proof of being heard.

AMAZIAH.

Stop the baldheaded prater's ribald tongue,
Nor longer let him vent his blasphemies!
He hath profaned the awful name, at which
The world adores and trembles. Wizard hoar!
Thy counter-prayers and secret arts prevail
Against a nation's warm devotions. Here,
Here see the fatal cause of this long drought!
No wonder that the angry god withholds
His favor, whilst that this blasphemer lives.
We have besieged his throne; with flocks and herds
Incessantly his altar-fires have smoked,
And all in vain. Behold the guilty cause!
The god demands a human sacrifice,
And richer blood, his chiefest enemy's,
Must flow, and now, that he may be appeased.
Haste, seize the traitor, bind his aged limbs,
And lay him as a victim on the stone!

ALL.

Down with the wretch! kill him! away with him!
Let not his presence more pollute the earth!

AMAZIAH.

Our royal master sees the people's rage;
It swelleth like the sea, nor can be curbed.
Will he not yield consent?

JEZEBEL.

I give my voice,
To have this insolent wretch at once cut off.

MAACHAH.

The gloomy bigot! let him die the death.

HIEL.

Aye, crush the reptile, on him stamp the heel,
And leave no fragment to all future time.

AHAB.

My lords and ladies! much it irketh me
To say ye nay; but I have pledged my word,
Safe-conduct have engaged.   It must be kept.

AMAZIAH.

And suffer vile blasphemers to escape!
What rights of faith preserved, or promises,
Can outlaws claim, the enemies avowed
Of God and man?

HIEL.

Spare not the snivelling dotard!
Smite the conspirator against thy peace,
The troubler of the realm!

3*

ITHOBAL.

I thank the gods,
For this propitious hour! Thine influence add,
O queen! of him thou hatest rid thyself!

JEZEBEL.

Art thou a king, and dost thou yet allow
Petty punctilios to restrain thy hands?
Kings are above all law; the fountains they
Of honor; in the place of God they stand;
Their doings none may question or gainsay.

AHAB.

My noble lords! the royal word is pledged.
To all my faults I dare not add this crime,
Dishonored in the world's eyes and mine own.
And since this trial should approach its close,
And Baal's priests the livelong day have prayed,
It is but just the prophet in his turn
Now offer sacrifice; and if so be,
No answering sign from heaven be vouchsafed,
As he this convocation first proposed,
I to your pleasure will surrender him.
Heralds! make room, all needful things provide.

ELIJAH.

Countrymen, Hebrews, Sons of Israel,
Of him who, as a prince, had power with God!

If any faithful and devout remain
In all this concourse, let him hither come,
And build with me an altar to the Lord.
I charge you by those grand old memories
Which cluster round our nation's history.
Can you forget the wonders and the signs;
- The land of bondage, and the pilgrim march;
The pillared cloud; the separated sea;
The thundered law, and Sinai in a blaze;
The manna and the rock; the swollen flood
Of Jordan parted in the midst; the walls
Of Jericho at seventh circuit fall'n;
The giant Anakim, the banded kings,
Vanquished by Israel's victorious arms?
Can ye forget, O Israel! who nursed
Your weakness into strength, on eagle-wings
Upbare you, like a mother overwatched
And to your present greatness led your steps?
Will you forsake Jehovah, Lord of Hosts?

Upon this height, by hands of godly men,
In generations past, an altar rose
To the true God. Dismantled and broke down,
Ours be it now this ruin to repair.
Set up twelve stones on which no tool hath passed,
According to the number of the tribes,
And dig around the base a shallow trench.
Next pile the wood; the bullock kill and flay;
And all his pieces place upon the wood:

It is a whole burnt-offering to the Lord.
Wherefore, to testify his world-wide rule,
I wave the shoulder to the north, whence come
Frost or fair weather, as his breath directs;
Unto the south, impregned with softening winds;
Unto the east, that hails the rising sun;
Unto the west, that sees its going down.
And now, to silence scoffing lips, that fain
Would prate of juggling and collusive arts,
Four water-barrels empty on the whole.
A second time repeat it; and a third;
Until both altar, sacrifice, and wood,
Are saturated, and the trench o'erflows.

ZABDIEL.

Oh, how my heart did leap to hear his words,
As though it had with holy fire been touched!
Dost note the slanting shadows?   'Tis the hour
Of evening sacrifice, by the old law
Appointed.

HEZRON.

True! a strange coincidence!

ZABDIEL.

And dost thou note the man of God his face
Studious averteth from the sun, to teach
The crowd, the god they worship is not his?

HEZRON.

And see ! he stretcheth forth his hands to pray.
Believest thou that fire will fall from heaven ? .

ZABDIEL.

If there's a God in Israel, it will.

ELIJAH.

O Thou Most High Jehovah, cov'nant God
Of holy Abraham, Isaac, Israel !
The hour hath come for thee to pluck thine hand
From out thy bosom, and to bare thine arm
In sight of all the people.   Let them know
That thou art Israel's God, worthy alone
Of praise and worship, working in the heavens
As pleases thee, and ruling over all.
Approve me as thy servant, and make known
That all that I have done was at thy word,
And not of mine own counsel.   Hear me, Lord,
O hear ! and answer by a sign of dread.
As thou didst Aaron, Gideon, David, hear;
That they may know thou art Jehovah-God,
For thy name jealous, yet most merciful.

HEZRON.

See ! see ! the fire of heaven ! from the clear sky
The flash descends—the altar's in a blaze—
The sacrifice is hid in smoke—the wood,

The stones, the very dust, are all consumed,
All melted in one mass of blood-red flame—
Ne'er for such purpose to be used again.
And see! the water hissing in the trench,
The fire hath licked it up, to vapor turned.

ELIJAH.

Down on your faces, O ye people, fall,
And own your God! the great Jehovah own!

ALL.

Behold a miracle! a miracle!
Jehovah is the God, the God alone;
Jehovah is the true and living God.
No more we worship idols, but our backs
We turn on Baal, and the Lord adore.

ELIJAH.

Now if ye from your idols truly turn,
And will be zealous for the Lord of Hosts,
Seize the false priests of Baal, let none flee!
So is it written in the law, " If one,
Although he be thy bosom-friend, and dear
As thine own soul, should slily thee entice
To follow other gods, thou shalt not spare,
Nor shall thine eye have pity. He shall die,
For that he thrust thee from the Lord away,
Who brought thee from the land of bondage." Hence!

Away with the idolatrous, foul brood,
To Kishon's brook, and slay them there. The waves
Shall wash the land forever of this plague.

JEZEBEL.

Wilt thou, O king, permit this massacre
Of a whole priestly tribe, before thine eyes ?

AHAB.

I cannot interfere. Such was the pact,
Such the conditions I myself imposed,
" Failure, to either party fatal proves."

ZEPHON.

It may be weakness, but such bloody scenes
Are to my feelings most repugnant. Truth
Requires not, sure, such questionable aids.
Not words of thunder, nor rebukes of fire,
Not earthquake throes, nor elemental war,
But gentle ministries of patient love,
Subdue the heart, and melt its flint to tears.

OBADIAH.

The fickle people and the court, I know
Better than those who in seclusion live,
And premature this exultation deem.
Sudden reforms, unbased on principle,
Lack root and permanence. Reaction comes ;
The cloud exhales before the first hot sun ;

The unfed torrent dies out in the sand;
Discouragement ensues, despair and fear.
Stunned by the failure and the total wreck,
Ev'n prophets, for they are but men, may yield
The hopeless cause, and to the desert flee.

ELIJAH.

In the faint rustle of the leaves, O king!
I hear the token of returning grace;
Now get thee up, to thy pavilion hie,
And with unwonted gladness spread the feast.
I give myself to prayer.   Thou, Zephon! climb
Yon rising ground, and bring me sure report
What thou discernest on the rough'ning sea.

God of my fathers! let me with thee plead;
Appear for thine own name; thy word fulfil;
Nor leave thy cause to deep reproach and shame!

ZEPHON.

No pleasing change I mark: the brazen sky
Glows with unshaded and relentless glare.

ELIJAH.

Seven times return again, and watch untired.

O gracious King of Heaven! shall the bold mocks
Of heathen scoffers now insult mine ear,

While they profanely cry, " Where is thy God ?
Not for mine honor, Lord ! but thy great name,
Reveal thine arm, and teach the godless world,
'Tis Thou alone, not Gentile vanities,
That rain dost give, from out thy treasure-cloud.

ZEPHON.

Seven times mine eye hath the far sea-line swept,
Since thou hast here bowed motionless, thine head
Deep-buried in thine hands : and now at length
Out of the sea ascends a little cloud
In form and bigness like a human hand.

ELIJAH.

I thank thee, God of prayer !   On rapid wing
Expanding, 'twill o'ercanopy the heavens,
And burst with sudden and resistless force
In an impetuous deluge on the plain.
My lord, O king ! thy chariot prepare,
That the swift-coming tempest stay thee not;
Whiles that thy servant, girding up his loins,
Will run before thee to thy palace-gate.

Welcome, thrice welcome, to the thirsty fields,
The genial gift of Him who answers prayer !
Praise to the King of Glory ! who doth give
Unto his saints a two-edged sword, his wrath
To execute upon the heathen, and to bind

In chains the rebels that oppose his will.
Sons of the prophets ! lead the swelling strain,
For this should be a joyful day to you.

Chorus of the Sons of the Prophets.[30]

I.

Laud, blessing, adoration, are thy right,
 Great King of boundless majesty !
Thy mantle is the living light ;
Thou fillest heaven's high throne,
And sway'st the sceptre of the skies alone :
 Among the gods none dares to rival thee.

II.

Thou madest heaven and earth,
 The hoarse waves echo back thine awful name ;
Thou wast, before the mountains had their birth,
 Before the pillars of old Nature's frame.

III.

The flaming sun
 Thy glory, not his own, reveals ;
 As on his swift but silent wheels,
 Along the constellated arch,
 With giant step, and conqueror's march,
He slackens not the rein, until his goal be won.

IV.

Rising, setting,
Ne'er forgetting
The place to which he, panting, must return;
Thy guiding will
He hastens to fulfil,
'Which formed him first, and bade his splendors burn.

V.

The thunder is thy voice; and thine, O God!
The lightning's terrible beauty, gleaming far;
When thou dost yoke the whirlwind to thy car,
And ride upon the wings of storms abroad.

IV

O'er the Great Sea resounds the deafening roar,
The range of Lebanon it rolleth o'er,
And Sirion shakes at its terrific peals.
Flash after flash the forest-depths reveals,
Shivers the lofty cedars with its stroke,
And of its foliage strips the giant oak.
Rent is the black and overhanging pall,
And welcome torrents on the valleys fall.

VII.

What are idols, false and vain?
Lust and blood are in their train;

Sightless eyes and helpless hands;
None his votary understands;
Weak to bless, and weak to ban,
Senseless god, and senseless man!

VIII.

Our God is in the heavens: He guides
The starry paths, the ocean tides;
Nothing too great, nothing too small!
His equal eye is over all;
Dropping with gold the insect's wing,
Or widest empires managing.
The callow raven's cry he hears,
And champion of the poor appears.

IX.

They that persecute the just
  Touch the apple of his eye;
  His terrors make th' oppressor fly,
And beat the wicked small as dust.
    Though hand in hand,
    The wicked band,
  His people to exterminate;
    For Israel's sighs
    He will arise,
  Their righteous cause to vindicate.
    Asunder cut the impious cords,
    God of gods, and Lord of lords!

X.

Praise Him in the highest height,
Lucid orbs of quenchless light!
Praise Him in the depths below,
Lightning's flash, and winter's snow!

Praise Him, mountains gray and tall;
Torrents, that in thunder fall!
Birds, whose song the morning wakes;
Beasts, whose roar the forest shakes!

Praise Him, ye of mortal race,
Sharers of his sevenfold grace;
Gifts of mercy, deeds of power,
Witnessed by each grateful hour!

Praise Him, princes on the throne;
Praise Him, tribes of every zone!
Join, O Earth! thy loftiest hymn
To the chant of Cherubim!

[Exeunt Omnes.

(1.) *The sacred car of ivory and gold.*

Compare the description of Solomon's chariot, Song, iii. 10. See also Xenophon's account of the white chariot and horses of the Sun, *Cyrop.* bk. 8, c. xix., and the similar account of Herodotus, bk. 8, c. lv. ; and 2 Kings xxiii. 11.

(2.) *The Virgins of the Sun thou dost perceive.*

The attaching of women as part of the corps of the temple has always been common in idolatrous countries. The Vestal Virgins of the Romans were indeed bound by solemn vows to a life of chastity, and were buried alive if detected in a transgression. They were released from their vows at thirty years of age, and permitted to marry. Their office was to tend the perpetual fire, day and night. "Esta," says Chevalier Ramsay, "is a Chaldee word which signifies fire, and from thence comes the Greek word Estia. The Romans added V to it, and made it Vesta, as of Espera they made Vespera."—*Travels of Cyrus*, p. 29, note. But of the Dancing-girls who are found attached to every Hindoo temple, it is no calumny to say that they are any thing but Vestal Virgins. "The first in rank are the sacrificers, whose duties are numerous and daily. Next in importance are the Devadassi or handmaids of the gods ; they have the charge of the sacred lamps, and generally are concubines to the Brahmins, and, in fact, low and abandoned in their morals. They dance and sing the impure songs in which the licentious actions of their gods are celebrated. These persons are sometimes dedicated to this life by their parents, and are not considered as reflecting any disgrace on the family to which they belong. They are the only females who learn to read, to sing, and to dance. Such accomplishments are held in abhorrence by all the virtuous matrons of India."—Malte-Brun's Univ. Geogr. ii. 243. The priestesses of Venus in Corinth were of a like character. The famous Lais was of the number.

It would seem that the worship of the groves among the Syrians, and imitated by the Jews, had the same adjuncts. Josiah, among his other reforms, "brake down the houses of consecrated persons, *hakkedeshim* (the term is applied in the Scriptures only to the vilest individuals), that were by the house of the Lord, where the women wove hangings for the grove." These women were employed to make rich and costly garments for the shrine, or to dress the image itself; unless we take the word "hangings," with Michaelis, to mean curtains or tents for the concealment of the worshippers. In the Iliad, Hecuba is advised by Hector to select her finest peplum, as a present to propitiate Minerva.—Iliad, vi. 271.

> "The largest mantle your full wardrobes hold,
> Most priz'd for art, and labor'd o'er with gold,
> Before the Goddess' honor'd knees be spread."

(3.) *They the Chemarim are.*

The passage in 2 Kings xxiii. 4–14, already alluded to, is rich in suggestions. "*The idolatrous priests* whom the kings of Judah had appointed to burn incense in the high places," and who seem to be different from the priests of Baal (for it is added, "them *also* that burned incense unto Baal, to the sun, and to the moon, and to the planets, and to all the host of heaven"), are in the original called *Chemarim*, so called according to Kimchi, because they wore black clothes. This was a remarkable contrast, for the priests of Jehovah were required to wear white linen. These priests, from the circumstance of being robed in black, may be supposed to be dedicated to the infernal powers.

The *Casdim* are Chaldeans. The name of the nation became appropriated to that class who dealt in occult studies, as we call a fortune-teller a Gipsy, and the French, a Bohemian. The whole people seem to have had a passion for astrological studies, fostered by the tower of Belus, and the observatory on which Callisthenes found observations recorded for 1903 years, till within fifteen years of the time when the tower was built. Prideaux' Conn. i. 123. Curtius narrates that "*Chaldæi Vates*" warned Alexander not to enter Babylon at his peril. "Chaldæi, non ex artis, sed ex gentis, vocabulo nominati, predicere dicuntur, quoquisque fate natus esset."—Cic. de Divin. i.

The *Chartummim* are the "*magicians*" of Daniel ii. 2. The word denotes *sacred scribes ;* they were perhaps students of the secrets of nature, including the idea of genethliacs, or casters of nativities. In Daniel the nice distinctions between the various grades of magicians, astrologers (*ashaphim*, whence the *sophoi* of the Greeks), sorcerers, and Chaldeans, may be traced to advantage by the critical student. See *Poli Synopsis, in loc.*

(4.) *The Prophets of the Grove, full twenty score,*
  Are absent.

The absence of the prophets of the Grove, who were particularly embraced in the challenge of Elijah, is worth noticing. The reason of their absence must be left entirely to conjecture. Perhaps, as they were a sort of domestic chaplains of the queen, "which eat at Jezebel's table," and so were under her special patronage, they were not subject to Ahab's direct orders ; or Jezebel may have detained them from prudential considerations : or some punctilio of etiquette or precedence may have kept them from joining with the priests of Baal.

The word *Asherah*, translated *Grove*, is capable of being rendered Astarte ; and this rendering is preferred by Theodoret and Selden, De Dis Syris, 2, c. ii. p. 232. As early as the time of Solomon the worship of "Ashtoreth the abomination of the Zidonians," had been introduced. When Ahab married his Zidonian wife, to gratify her he not only "raised an altar for Baal in the house of Baal, which he had built in Samaria," but he "made a grove," or rather, he made an image of Ashtoreth or Astarte, his wife's goddess, conveniently near, 1 Kings xvi. 33.

4

(5.) *The Syrian Goddess.*

The principal authority to be consulted in regard to the mythology of the Syrians, is Lucian, the eminent sophist and satirist. Being a native of Samosata, a city of Syria, not far from the Euphrates, although of Greek ancestry, he was in the habit of calling himself a Syrian or Assyrian. He flourished in the reign of Trajan, and of course is incompetent to testify of what passed a thousand years before; and his derivation of the Eunuch-priests called Galli from the story of Combabus and Stratonice, wife first of Seleucus and afterward of Antiochus, shows a date six hundred years later than the time of Ahab. Still it cannot be doubted that some of the traditions which he cited may be depended on, and particularly the account of the Syrian buildings, deities, and worship. Such an account he undertook to give in a dissertation "concerning the Syrian Goddess." From this treatise, which is known only to scholars, two or three extracts may be acceptable. It is worthy of note that Lucian explicitly affirms that the Assyrians borrowed from the Egyptians their traditions concerning the gods.

"There is also another great temple in Phœnicia, held by the Sidonians, which they say was erected to Astarte; by which Astarte, I suppose, they mean the Moon: however, one of the priests told me, that it belonged to Europa, the sister of Cadmus. . . . . . I saw likewise a temple in Byblis, dedicated to Venus [Aphrodite] Byblia, wherein they perform sacred rites to Adonis, and I was instructed in the same. They relate, that the misfortune of Adonis, who was slain by a boar, happened in their country; and, in memory thereof, whip themselves every year, mourning, and performing many ceremonies; at which time great lamentation is made by them over all the country; but, when they have done whipping themselves and lamenting, in the first place, they offer up funeral sacrifices to. Adonis, as being dead; but then, on the morrow after, they feign he is restored to life again, and ascended up through the air into heaven, when they shave their heads, as the custom of the Egyptians is upon the death of Apis; but for those women that will not have their heads shaved, this is the penalty inflicted on them; they are to stand one whole day, and expose their bodies to sale only to strangers; and the money that they get by so doing, is offered up as a present to Venus. But there are some of the Byblians who say, that Osiris the Egyptian was buried amongst them, and that all their lamentation and solemnity is performed, not in honor of Adonis, but Osiris; in confirmation whereof they tell you this story, which makes it the more probable. They say a head is brought every year from Egypt to Byblis, over the sea, in the space of seven days, the winds carrying it with such a divine gale, that it turneth neither to the one side nor to the other, but comes in a straight passage directly to Byblis; which, though it may seem miraculous, happens every year, and did the same when I was there; by which means I myself had a sight of the Byblian head."—*Dryden's Lucian,* vol. I. 242.

By Astarte Lucian understood the Moon. Ashteroth, says Selden, is Astarte in the LXX., and in the Alexandrine Chronicle, Eustarte. Rabbi David derives it from a word signifying sheep, as if from the number of offerings. Philastrius thinks Asthar the name of a man. Ashtoreth was a city in the kingdom of Bashan, Josh. xii. 4. Whether the city was called from the goddess, or the goddess from a city, is uncertain. The Philistines put Saul's armor in the house of Ashtaroth. The word is frequently rendered *grove.* As groves, like mountains, were favorite places of worship, may there not have been many goddesses worshipped under this name, as Jupiter Endendros of the Rhodians, and Diana Nemorosa?

But it is an objection to the translation, *grove* (though it has the sanction of Josephus), that it is a sense sometimes inconsistent with the connection; thus: "They set them up images and groves in every high hill, and under every green tree." 2 Kings xvii. 10. Surely they did not erect groves in groves, or a tree under a tree. Manasseh placed in the temple "a graven image of a grove, *Aserah,*" 2 Kings xxi. 7. This is said in close connection with his rearing up altars for Baal, and all the host of heaven. It was from the Sidonians that Ahab borrowed the chief deities Baal and Ashtoreth. But in the Sidonian or Syrian mythology, there is no other deity besides Ashtoreth or Astarte, ("Ashtoreth, the goddess of the Zidonians," 1 Kings xi. 5), the

Moon, called by such names as Asaroth, Asarim, or Asarah, nor is there any evidence of such a thing as a grove being worshipped under this name. The image might have been made of wood, and so have given rise to the ambiguity; as Josiah burnt Manasseh's image, and Gideon cut down the grove, or image, upon the altar. Wooden images, covered with gold, are mentioned by Isaiah and Jeremiah.

To return to Astarte:—this goddess is said to have borne, as the symbol of dominion, an ox's head, the horns of which indicated beams of light. A star, supposed to have fallen from heaven, was dedicated to her in Tyre. Cicero describes four goddesses who bore the same name, Juno, Venus, the Moon, and the mistress of Adonis. Chevalier Ramsay identifies the latter with Urania, the queen of stars, degraded to earth. Trav. of Cyrus, p. 185. Jahn coincides in the opinion that Astarte was the Moon. Archæol. § 409. According to Augustine, she was Juno. According to Euripides, she was Io. There can be no doubt, that as there were many Junos and Venuses, so there were many Astartes. Selden is in doubt whether Astarte is the same as Beltis or Baaltis. But as the Sun is the king of heaven, the Moon may appropriately be styled the queen of heaven.—Syntagma, II. p. 158.

Layard identifies her with Hera, or the Assyrian Venus; and adds, that the monuments hitherto discovered present no corroboration of the infamous law which, according to Herodotus, marked her rites at Babylon. "She was 'the Queen of Heaven' frequently alluded to in the sacred volumes. Diodorus mentions the vases which were placed on tables in the Babylonian temple; the prophet describes the drink-offerings to her; and in the sculptures, the king is constantly represented with a cup in one hand, in the act of performing some religious ceremony. The planet which bore her name, was sacred to her, and, in the Assyrian sculptures, a star is placed upon her head. She was called Beltis, because she was the female form of the great divinity, or Baal; the two, there is reason to conjecture, having been originally but one, and androgyne. Her worship penetrated from Assyria into Asia Minor, where its Assyrian origin was recognized. In the rock tablets of Pterium she is represented, as in those of Assyria, standing erect on a lion, and crowned with a tower, or mural coronet, which, we learn from Lucian, was peculiar to the Semitic figure of the goddess. This may have been a modification of the high cap of the Assyrian bas-reliefs. To the Shemites she was known under the names of Astarte, Ashtaroth, Mylitta, and Alitta, according to the various dialects of the nations amongst which her worship prevailed. . . . It has been conjectured that this name [Astarte] was derived from the word 'star' in the primitive Indo-European languages, from whence, it is well known, came the Persian female name Satara, the daughter of Darius, and that of the biblical Esther. . . . This custom of placing the figure of a star upon the heads of idols is probably alluded to by the prophet. 'The star of your god, which ye made to yourselves.' Amos v. 26."—Layard's Nineveh, vol. II. pp. 346, 347.

(6.) *Samaria's Temple-Palace.*

It is said of Ahab that after marrying Jezebel, the Sidonian, "he went and served Baal, and worshipped him. And he reared up an altar for Baal in the house of Baal, which he had built in Samaria. And Ahab made a grove."—1 Kings xvi. 32.

The Egyptians joined the palace and the temple together, thus surrounding the royal throne with the prestige of divine sanctity. The Assyrian custom seems to have been similar, at least no separate temples have yet been found among the exhumations. "As in Egypt, he [the king] may have been regarded as the representative, on earth, of the deity; receiving his power directly from the gods, and the organ of communication between them and his subjects. All the edifices hitherto discovered in Assyria, have precisely the same character; so that we have most probably the palace and temple combined: for in them the deeds of the king and of the nation, are united with religious symbols, and with the statues of the gods."—Layard's Nineveh, vol. II. p. 211.

Lucian's description of the great Phœnician temple of the Syrian goddess at Byblis, is as follows:

"The place itself, you must know, whereon the temple standeth, is the knoll of an hill, lying about the middle of the city, and hath a double wall encompassing it round; of which walls the one is ancient, and the other not much older than the age we live in. But the porch of the temple lieth towards the north, in circumference about one hundred fathoms, wherein the Pria-pusses [φαλλοι] stand, whom Bacchus dedicated, being three hundred cubits high, into one of which a man getteth up every year twice, and dwelleth seven days together at the top of the Phallus [to .pray nearer the gods]. . . . As for the temple, it looks towards the sun-rising, but its form and workmanship is after the same manner as the temples in Ionia. There stands a great basis of about two fathoms in height, whereon the tower is erected, to the which you go up by stone steps; and when you are once ascended, the porch before the temple is very admira-ble and delightful to the view, being adorned not only with golden doors, but the whole temple glistering exceedingly with gold, and the roof covered with the same; from whence you may perceive a divine fragrant scent, equal to the best odors in Arabia. Being ascended a great height, it emits a most pleasant smell, and the same likewise when you descend, insomuch that your garments for a long time after retain the scent, and you your-self cannot but always remember it. Within the chapel there is a temple [θαλαμος] with a small ascent to it; it hath no doors, but lieth always open. Now all enter into the great temple, but only the priests into the chapel; yet not all of them either, but such only as are nearest related to the gods, and devote their whole lives to the service of the temple. Herein are placed the statues of the gods, as Juno and Jupiter, whom they call by another name, of their own denomination. Both are of gold, and are made both sitting, but Juno is carried by lions, and Ju-piter by bulls. . . . I formerly mentioned, on the left hand, as you enter into the temple, there stands first the throne of the sun, but without any image of the sun itself; for the sun and moon only have no statues amongst them, and, as I understand, the ground thereof was this: they say, that it is a holy thing to erect statues to other gods, inasmuch as their forms are not manifest to us; but the sun and moon are evidently seen by all, wherefore it would be unnecessary to make the images of what we daily behold in the air. After this throne is placed the statue of Apollo, . . . with a long beard. . . . Whensoever he hath a mind to give answer, he first of all moveth himself in the seat, . . . if the thing proposed displeases him, he retires backward ; but if he approves of it, he then drives and hurries on his supporters forwards, as a coachman drives his horses ; and in this manner they collect his answers. . . . I will here also acquaint you with another thing, that happened while I was present. The priests, having lifted him up, throwing them down he quitted their shoulders, and walked himself in the air. Now after Apollo, the next is, the statue of Atlas, then Mercury, and then of Lucina ; which is the side-furniture of the temple : but without there standeth a great altar made of· brass, besides a thousand other brazen statues of kings and priests."—Dryden's Lucian, vol. I. p. 259–265. ·

For a description of the Temple of the Sun in Cuzco, the city of the Incas, the reader is referred to Prescott's History of Peru. A brief and graphic account of it is presented from the pen of an English traveller : " Where now stands the church of San Domingo, then rose that glorious fane, the Temple of the Sun, with its grand central door, and massive cornice of pure gold. The interior was decorated with a magnificence suited to the holy uses to which it was dedicated. A large golden sun, studded with emeralds and turquoises, covered the side facing the door ; a sacred flame constantly burned before the representative of the deity ; and vases of gold, a metal which the Incas believed to be 'the tears shed by the sun,' stood, filled with sacrificial first fruits, on the floor of the temple. The other sides of the Yntip-pampa were occupied by massive stone temples dedicated to Quilla, or the moon, in which all the utensils were of silver ; to Coyllur-cuna, or the hosts of heaven ; to Chasca, the planet Venus, called ' the youth with flowing golden locks ; ' to Ccuicha, or the rainbow ; and to Yllapa, or thunder and lightning. . . . The convent of the virgins of the Sun, called the aclla-huasi, was situated near the Yntip-pampa."—Markham's Cuzco, pp. 120, 123.

(7.) *Their silver helms with disc and crescent topped.*

Osburn, from a careful study of the wall-paintings of Egypt, has been enabled to reproduce a very satisfactory description of the Sidonian warriors. He says the Sidonians, "in personal appearance, were a fine muscular race. Their features resembled those of the Arvadites and Tyrians. Their statesmen and merchants wore the hair and beard long with the fillet round the head. Their warriors cut the hair, beard, and whiskers short. Their arms and accoutrements were worthy of the fame and riches of their great city. The helmet was of silver, with a singular ornament at the crown, consisting of a disc and two horns of a heifer or of the crescent moon. This symbol is not at all like any thing worn in Egypt, but strikingly resembles the horns of Astarte, on the coins and medals of Phœnicia. This disc was the badge of a prince. Inferior ranks were denoted by the two horns only. The armor consisted of plates of some white metal, probably silver, quilted upon a white linen garment, which was laced in front and reached up to the armpits, being supported by shoulder-straps. The shield was large and circular, like that of the Philistines. It was of iron rimmed with gold and ornamented with golden studs or bosses. The sword, which was of bronze, was two-edged, and shaped like the modern poniard. The spear was a long lance."—Osburn's Ancient Egypt, p. 119.

(8.) *And live queen Isabel!*

The sacred historian mentions it as an aggravation of Ahab's wickedness, that he took to wife the daughter of Ethbaal, or Ithobal, king of the Sidonians, and with her introduced her country's idols to the Israelites. Her name in the original Hebrew is *Izebel*, in the LXX., Iezebel, corresponding nearly to our modern *Isabel*, and much more euphonious than the name Jezebel; in which the *I* is hardened by Anglo-Saxon usage into *J*. According to Rollin, the Tyrian princess Dido was the grand-niece of Jezebel, being great-granddaughter of Ithobal, or Ethbaal, called by Josephus king of both Tyre and Sidon. There is nothing in the chronology to conflict with the opinion.

It will be perceived, that while I have (with Krummacher) depicted Ahab as an easy, weak, capricious monarch, addicted to sensual pleasures, but not naturally either ambitious or cruel; I have represented Jezebel as a beautiful, fascinating, accomplished, ambitious, and unscrupulous woman, just such as were

Cleopatra, Catharine of Guise, Mary, queen of Scots, and Lady Macbeth. That with her great administrative qualities she had Queen Elizabeth's personal vanity is inferrible from her painting her face and tiring her head when about to present herself before Jehu.

(9.) *Of Carmel's well-pois'd mount.   Garden of God !*

The most satisfactory description of Mount Carmel is to be found in Stanley's "Sinai and Palestine." According to this writer, the mountains of Palestine are generally bare and rugged. Mount Carmel is one of the rare exceptions, being covered with verdure to its very summit. It is this feature which gave it its name, *Carm-El*, "the Garden of God." It owes its distinction to its beauty rather than its loftiness; for it is nowhere higher than 1,700 feet above the level of the sea. It is a long mountain range, extending eighteen miles from the interior, and terminating in a bluff promontory. This promontory, which, from its historical associations, has monopolized the name, boldly overlooks the Levant, opposite Acre (the old Accho); and is surrounded by a broad beach, easily traversed by the successive armies of the Philistines, Egyptians,.and Crusaders. The bay, bounded by Carmel on the south and by the hills of Galilee on the north, forms the embouchure of the great plain, or battle-field of Esdraelon.

The commanding position of the promontory is alluded to by Jeremiah : "Surely as Tabor is among the mountains, and as Carmel is by the sea, so shall the king of Babylon come." Jer. xxvi. 18. The luxuriance and fertility of the mountain are indicated in various passages of Holy Writ. Isaiah celebrates "the excellency of Carmel and Sharon." Isa. xxxv. 2. To an Israelite, says Stanley, it seemed like a natural park ; it was a type and standard of beauty, and its sterility was the consummation of misfortune. "The top of Carmel shall wither." Amos i. 2. "The earth mourneth and languisheth ; Lebanon is ashamed and hewn down ; Sharon is like a wilderness ; and Bashan and Carmel shake off their fruits." Isa. xxxiii. 9. When cultivated, as in the time of Uzziah, who had "vine-dressers" there (2 Chron. xxvi. 10), and adorned with vineyards, groves of olives, and

4*

orchards of almond and fig-trees, it might well deserve its name.

Hence we see the appropriateness of likening to it the ornaments of an Eastern bride, "thy head upon thee is like Carmel." Solomon's Song, vii. 5. Carne says that no mountain in Palestine retains so much of its ancient beauty as this.—Letters from the East, vol. II. 119. Van Richter describes it as "entirely covered with verdure : on its summit are pines and oaks;'and farther down olives and laurel-trees. Many odoriferous flowers, as hyacinths, jonquilles, tazettes, anemones, &c., grow wild upon the mountain. From it issue a multitude of brooks emptying into the Kishon, the largest of which is the so-called fountain of Elijah."—See Robinson's Calmet, Art. Carmel.

It has been supposed that when Amos said, "though they hide themselves in the top of Carmel," Amos ix. 3, he meant the caves or grottoes, which are numerous and intricate; in some of which Obadiah may have concealed the Lord's prophets, ("an hundred prophets, and hid them by fifty in a cave," 1 Kings xviii. 4,) and which were the favorite resort of both Elijah and Elisha. But we are assured, that there are no caves in the summit, though there are very large ones under the western cliffs. Hence the language of the prophet must be referred to the thick vegetation, which would furnish a sufficient screen.—Mission of Inq. to the Jews, p. 235. Sinai and Pal. p. 345.

The view, in every direction from the top of the mountain, is magnificent. "Mount Carmel," says Lamartine, "begins to rise, at some minutes' walk from Kaïpha. We climbed it, by a tolerably good road, cut in the rock, on the very edge of the promontory; every step we ascended discovered to us a new prospect of the sea, of the hills of Palestine, and the borders of Idumea."—Pilgr. to the Holy Land, vol. I. 209. The view takes in the plain of Esdraelon, the winding Kishon, the site of Jezreel, and Samaria, with Mount Tabor and Great Hermon, which Lieut. Lynch saw covered with snow in June.—See Official Report, 4to, p. 116.

The geological character of the mountains of Syria was carefully examined by Dr. Anderson, who accompanied Lynch's exploring party. They are of secondary and later limestones, with basaltic and tertiary interruptions, once covered by the waters of the great Jurassic Ocean. A few miles from the convent on Mt. Carmel, are found remarkable petrifactions known as "Elijah's melons," said by the legends to be fruit turned into stone by the prophet, to punish the refusal of the owner to supply his wants. These quartz nodules, pebbles, or "turk's-heads," are round and smooth, and were used by Djezzar Pasha for cannon balls.—Stanley, p. 153. Lynch's Off. Rept. p. 95.

The botanical features of Mt. Carmel were observed by Dr. Griffith. He noticed the following specimens: *Ranunculaceæ;* Adonis autumnalis, common from Mt. Carmel and Nazareth to the sources of Jordan, with varieties in the tints. *Malvaceæ;* Lavatera thuringiniana, at the foot of the mountain. *Fabaceæ;* Genista monosperma, the Rotem of the Arabs, and Juniper of the Bible, its roots unfit for food. (But Bonar insists that it is broom. Desert of Sinai, p. 389.) *Asteraceæ;* Helychrysum Orientale. *Solanaceæ;* Mandragora autumnalis, or mandrake, Jiabora of the Arabs, the Dudaim of Genesis, and still valued for supposed aphrodisiac powers.—*Liliaceæ;* Asphodelus ramosus, or Asphodel.—Off. Rept. pp. 59–67.

Dr. Thomas Scott has supposed, and Dr. Robinson seems to favor the opinion, that the assembling of the priests took place at the base of the mountain. The commonly received opinion is that it occurred upon the summit, and the description may be explained in accordance with this belief. There had been an ancient altar there, 1 Kings xviii. 30 ; xix. 10, which Elijah repaired ; and it is not probable that an altar would have been erected except on the summit, in conformity with the prevalent passion for "high places." It is said also that Elijah brought the prophets of Baal "*down* to the brook Kishon, and slew them there." He bade Ahab prepare his chariot, and get him *down.* When it is afterward said, that "Elijah went *up* to the top of Carmel," this may easily be understood either of his returning thither after the slaughter at Kishon, or of his going to a higher eminence than was occupied by king Ahab.

Mr. Stanley's views on this point are worthy of notice. He argues that the scene of the sacrifice could never have been the spot occupied by the modern convent, but one more remote, according to tradition. "But be the tradition good or bad, the localities adapt themselves to the event in almost every particular. The summit thus marked out is the extreme eastern point of the range, commanding the last view of the sea behind, and the first view of the great plain in front, just where the glades of forest, the 'excellency of Carmel' sink into the usual barrenness of the hills and vales of Palestine. There on the highest point of the mountain, may well have stood, on its sacred 'high place,' the altar of the Lord, which Jezebel, had cast down. (The rocky fragments lying around, would naturally afford the materials for the 'twelve stones' of which the natural altar was built.) Close beneath, on a wide upland sweep, under the shade of ancient olives, and round a well of water, said to be perennial—and which may, therefore, have escaped the general drought, and have been able to furnish water for the trenches round the altar—must have been ranged, on the one side the king and people, with the 850 prophets of Baal and Astarte, and on the other side the solitary and commanding figure of the Prophet of the Lord. Full before them opened the whole plain of Esdraelon, with Tabor and its kindred ranges in the distance; on the rising ground, at the opening of its valley, the city of Jezreel, with Ahab's palace and Jezebel's temple distinctly visible; in the nearer foreground, immediately under the base of the mountain, was clearly seen the winding stream of the Kishon, working its way through the narrow pass of the hills into the Bay of Acre."—Sinai and Pal. p. 346.

Dr. Thomson, familiar, as a missionary, with every nook of Palestine, agrees with Mr. Stanley in assigning, as the scene of the sacrifice, the traditional spot called El Mukhrakah, or *the place of burning*, near the ruined village of El Mansurah. In the absence of rival claims, and coinciding, as it does, with "the altar in the open air, without a temple or even a statue," where, according to Josephus, Vespasian offered sacrifice, the tradition seems worthy of credit.—See The Land and the Book, II. p. 223.

(10.) *Lo! nature's priest, majestic Lebanon.*
"Lebanon closes the Land of Promise on the north, as the

Peninsula of Sinai on the south, but with this difference, that Lebanon, though beyond the boundaries of Palestine, is almost always within view. . . . The ancient names of its double range are all significant of this position. It was 'Sion,' 'the upraised;' or 'Hermon,' 'the lofty peak,' or 'Shenir' and 'Sirion,' the glittering 'breastplate of ice;' or above all, 'Lebanon,' the 'Mont Blanc' of Palestine; 'the White Mountains' of ancient times; the mountain of the 'Old White-headed man,' or the 'Mountain of Ice' in modern times. So long as its snowy tops were seen, there was never wanting to the Hebrew poetry the image of unearthly grandeur, which nothing but perpetual snow can give. The 'dews' of the mists that rose from its watery ravines, or of the clouds that rested on its summit, were perpetual witnesses of freshness and coolness, the sources, as it seemed, of all the moisture, which was to the land of Palestine what the fragrant oil was to the garments of the High Priest; what the refreshing influence of brotherly love was to the whole community. And deep within the recesses of the mountain, beneath its crest of ice and snow, was the sacred forest of cedars, famous, even to those who had never seen them, for their gigantic magnificence, endeared to the heart of the nation by the treasures thence supplied to the Temple and the Palace of Jerusalem."—Stanley's Sinai and Pal. p. 395.

(11.) *Chaldean numbers, big with coming fate.*

The Orientals have always had, and still have, a great passion for divination, magic, and the interpretation of dreams. Sortilege was a universal practice. Auguries from birds were obtained by observing their flight, whether to the right or left hand, their singing, and their eating or not eating. The use of arrows is alluded to in Ezekiel, ch. xxi. 21, when the king of Babylon, besides inspecting images or teraphim, and inspecting the livers of beasts, is described as also deciding on the direction of his march at the parting of two ways, by the use of arrows, in Hebr. *sons of the quiver.* Probably arrows inscribed with the names of certain cities which he proposed to attack, as Rabbah, Jerusalem, &c., were placed in a quiver, and shaken together, and the name drawn out decided his movements.

The Chaldean, or Babylonian numbers, were also in high

repute. They were astrological calculations. Horace warns against their use: "Nec Babylonios tentaris numeros." Ausonius also speaks of "cœli numeros et conscia sidera fati." Tacitus denounced them under the title of mathematicians, "mathematicos;" and Tiberius banished them from Rome. He was careful, however, to discriminate between the calculating Genethliacs and the Geometers. From Lieut. Burnes we learn that the Tartars will not start on a journey till the astrologers have pronounced the hour lucky. The Chinese are grossly addicted to this art, making use of what are known as the Eight Diagrams, invented by the Emperor Fuh-hi, more than 3,000 years before Christ. These have been multiplied into 64, the mines of wisdom in which have never been explored. Many books have been written in explanation, the most noted of which is a work in six volumes. The responses are obtained by studying the various combinations of the 64 diagrams, which are affected by the objects sought, and the meaning of the characters designating the current month and day. The characters have also a mysterious connection with the five elements, metal, wood, water, fire, and earth. If the character representing the day of birth is connected with wood, and that representing the month with metal, the augury is unfortunate, for metal cuts wood. But if one of the characters is connected with water, the result will be auspicious, because water promotes the growth of wood. The diviner is a shrewd fellow, and by a series of astute questions, finds out how to adapt his answers to his questioner. Then the events of a man's life are under the influences of 28 stars, each of which is an object of worship. They are traced on the periphery of the horoscope, and with the aid of the eight diagrams, determine the fortunes of the year, the month, or the day. The expense of these calculations sometimes amounts to several dollars.—See Nevius's Letters on the Religion and Superstitions of China, Lett. xiii. (Home and For. Record, Oct. 1858.)

(12.) *Round and round in mystic ring,*
Choir of planets symbolling.
Pope's lines will readily recur to mind,

" As eastern priests in giddy circles run,
And turn their heads to imitate the sun."

"The Egyptians had their solemn dances as well as the Jews;[*] the principal was their astronomical dance; of which the sacrilegious dance round the golden calf was an imitation."—Hor. Smith's Festivals, Games, &c., p. 195

(13.) *First the courier of the dawn*
Wakes the lark upon the lawn.

As Linnæus constructed a clock of flowers, according to the time of day when they expanded their blossoms, so a German woodsman is said to have invented an ornithological clock. The earliest riser seems to be the chaffinch, whose song precedes the dawn, being heard in summer from half past 1 to 2 o'clock. From 2 to half past 2, comes the black-cap; from half past 2 to 3, the quail; from 3 to half past 3, the hedge-sparrow; from half past 3 to 4, the blackbird; from 4 to half past 4, the lark, which has hitherto monopolized, without title, the credit of giving the earliest signal. From half past 4 to 5, the tit-mouse is heard, and last, and laziest of all, from 5 to half past 5, the sparrow.

(14.) *And thou shouldst be a king indeed.*

"The Rev. John Welch, a Scottish exile, was chosen pastor of a French Protestant congregation in St. Jean de Angely. This is the same Welch who married a daughter of John Knox, and of whom King James exclaimed when he heard it, 'Knox and Welch! the devil never made such a match as that.' 'It's right like, sir," replied Mrs. Welch, 'for we never speired his advice.' Louis XIII. having besieged and taken the town in which Welch ministered, and which he had been active in defending, summoned him into his presence to vindicate himself for preaching contrary to law in a place where the court was resident. 'Sir,' replied Welch, 'if your Majesty knew what I preached, you would not only come and hear it yourself, but make all France to hear it; for I preach not as those men you use to hear. First, I preach that you must be saved by the merits of Jesus Christ, and not your own; and I am sure your conscience tells you that your good works will never merit heaven. Next, I preach that, as you are king of France, there is no man on earth above you. But these men whom you hear subject you to the pope of Rome, which I will never do.' Pleased with this reply, Louis said to him, ' *He bien, vous serez mon ministre*—very good, you shall be my minister ;' and, addressing him by the title of 'father,' assured him of his protection. He was as good as his word ; for, in 1621, when the town was again besieged, he gave directions to take care of his minister, and he was safely conveyed with his family to Rochelle."— McCrie's Sketches of Scot. Hist., I. p. 176.

(15.) *Who feareth God can have no meaner fear.*

The admirer of Racine may be reminded of that beautiful and celebrated line in Athalie :

" Je crains Dieu, cher Abner, et n'ai point d'autre crainte."

(16.) *Ev'n Abraham, their vaunted patriarch,*
        A Chaldean was, and worshipper of fire.

Abraham emigrated from Ur of the Chaldees, a city of Mesopotamia, now called Orfah, but anciently Edessa. "Ur (Hebr. Oor), signifies light and fire, and, as the Chaldees were idolaters, this place might have been thus denominated from the sacred fire of their worship."—Bush's Q. and N. on Genesis, p. 132. "The Jews have a fable concerning the death of Haran : they say that Terah was not only an idolater, but a maker and seller of images ; and that one day going abroad, he left his son Abraham in the shop to sell them, who, during his father's absence, broke them all to pieces, except one ; upon which, when Terah returned and found what was done, he had him before Nimrod, who ordered him to be cast into a burning furnace, and he would see whether the God he worshipped would come and save him ; and whilst he was in it, they asked his brother Haran in whom he believed ? He answered, if Abraham overcomes, he would believe in his God, but if not, in Nimrod : wherefore they cast him into the furnace, and he was burnt ; and with respect to this it is said, *and Haran died before the face of Terah his father ;* but Abraham came out safe before the eyes of them all."—Gill on Gen. xi. 28. This is one of the Talmudical legends clumsily designed to explain a difficulty which does not exist, for the obvious meaning is, that Haran died in his father's lifetime, and it is, without doubt, in part borrowed from a like feat of Gideon, the young Iconoclast, which gave him the name of Jerubbaal, or the judge of Baal.—See Judg. vi. 27.

(17.) *Profoundest truths of astronomic lore.*

The close connection of the astronomy and the mythology of the Ethnics cannot have escaped the notice of the most cursory student of antiquity; how much they were mutually indebted to each other it is not easy to decide. See Origen contra Celsum, lib. I. p. 11. Instead of troubling the reader with attempts to reconcile the discrepancies of the various legends about Adonis or Tammuz, suffice it to say, that I have adhered to the simple and popular story, as it is told in every classical dictionary. The death and revivification of Adonis was exalted into an astronomical myth, adumbrating the alternations of winter and summer. Adonis, Baal, Bel, Tammuz, Apollo, or Hercules, is the same as the sun. Astarte or Ashteroth is the moon. Gesenius has devoted much learning to prove that Baal was the planet Jupiter, and Astarte the planet Venus. This might have been so in later times, but originally it is scarcely to be doubted that the sun and moon, as above designated, were worshipped as the generative and productive powers of nature. We find these two powers or principles still worshipped by the Hindoos. Much may be found on this whole subject, especially in regard to Urania and Adonis in Chev. Ramsay's Travels of Cyrus, Bk. vii. pp. 183–194.

As to the identity of Osiris and Adonis, see an ancient epigram preserved by Warburton, Div. Leg. of Moses, Bk. iv. Sec. 5 :

> " Ogygia me Bacchum vocat,
> Osirin Ægyptus putat,
> Mysi Phanacem nominant,
> Dionyson Indi existimant,
> Romana sacra Liberum,
> Arabica Gens Adoneum,
> Lucaniacus Pantheum."

(18.) *Who would th' city of palm-trees dare rebuild.*

Joshua, in his adjuration, did not say that Jericho should

never be rebuilt, but only pronounced a curse upon the builder.
Josh. vi. 26.   The literal fulfilment is recorded in 1 Kings xvi. 34.
Hiel is called the Bethelite.   Bethel was the southern seat of the
idolatry of the golden calves, and Hiel may well be supposed,
therefore, with a malignant hatred towards the Jewish religion.
As it is said, this was done in the reign of Ahab, "in his days;"
perhaps these words are meant to convey the idea, not merely of
synchronism, but of the royal concurrence and approbation.

(19.) *Sidon, the populous mart of all the world.*

Sidon, or Zidon, was a city of great antiquity.   It is supposed to have been founded soon after the Noachic deluge by
Sidon, the son of Canaan.   In the book of Joshua it is commemorated as "great Zidon."   It was allotted to the tribe of Asher,
but that tribe never succeeded in taking it.   The city of Laish
is said to have "dwelt careless, after the manner of the Zidonians, quiet and secure."   Judg. xviii. 7.   It is also mentioned
by Homer.   It was older than Tyre, which was its colony ; hence
Tyre is called "the daughter of Zidon."   Its commerce was ex-
tensive, and its merchants were princes.   The Sidonians have
the credit of inventing glass.   None were skilled like them to
carve in wood in the time of Solomon.   The famous Tyrian dye,
coveted by princes, was found in shell-fish taken off their coasts.
The richness of their military equipments has already been described in note, (p. 80).   Their superiority in the fine products
of the loom has been immortalized in the Iliad :

> " The Phrygian queen to her rich wardrobe went,
>   Where treasured odors breath'd a costly scent :
>   There lay the vestures of no vulgar art,
>   Sidonian maids embroidered every part."—Il. vi. 289.

Enriched by a vast commerce, Sidon long revelled in uninter-
rupted prosperity, as well as in that luxurious vice which is its
usual concomitant, though even Sidon had its Abdolonymus.   But
at length the thunder broke.   Prophet after prophet, Isaiah, Jeremiah, Ezekiel, Joel, Zechariah, denounced the wrath of Jehovah
against its heaven-daring impiety, and devoted it to ruin and de-
population.   In these predictions there is a nice discrimination

very worthy of notice, and which, by a singular oversight, escaped the keen eye of Keith, who, in his work on the prophecies, is totally silent upon Sidon. While in the prophecies against Tyre utter desolation is denounced, even to the minute prediction that it should be only a place for fishermen to spread their nets on, no such threat is to be found against Sidon. Her commerce was to dwindle, and her position to sink into insignificance, but no such entire disappearance is threatened as is against Tyre, "Thou shalt be sought for, yet thou shalt never be found again."—Ezek. xxiv. 21.

In remarkable accordance with this discrimination Tyre is at this day deserted save by a few fishermen; but Sidon, or Saida, is a small walled city of some 7,000 inhabitants, and it keeps up a petty trade in exports of fruits.—Prime's Trav. II. 321. It is well to bear this fact in mind, especially as Lamartine leaves the impression on his readers of the exact contrary: "Saïde, the ancient Sidon—a mere shadow of the ruined city, of which it has lost even the name—retaining no trace whatever of its past grandeur. A circular jetty formed of huge stones surrounds a haven filled with sand, from which a few fishermen and their children were pushing into the sea a frail bark without masts or sails— the sole maritime image remaining of this second queen of the seas."—Pilgr. I. 171. Dr. Robinson gives a much more satisfactory and circumstantial account: "The ancient harbor was formed by a long low ridge of rocks, parallel to the shore in front of the city. Before the time of Fakhr-ed-Din, there was here a port capable of receiving fifty galleys; but that chieftain, in order to protect himself against the Turks, caused it to be partly filled up with stones and earth; so that ever since his day only boats can enter it. Larger vessels lie without the entrance, on the north of the ledge of rocks, where they are protected from the south-west winds, but exposed to those from the northern quarter. . . . The commerce of Saida, which five and twenty years ago was still considerable, has of late years fallen off, in consequence of the prosperity of Beirût; the latter having become exclusively the port of Damascus. . . . The beauty of Saida consists in its gardens and orchards of fruit-trees, which fill the plain and extend to the foot of the adjacent hills." —Robinson's Bibl. Researches in Palestine, II. p. 478.

Although "the kings of Sidon" have long since been discrowned, Jer. v. 22; and "the strength of the sea" mourns over its fallen fortunes, Isa. xxiii. 4; Sidon is not abandoned to desolation. It is still prosperous on a small scale, and the exterior of the town presents "a most lovely appearance."—Paxton's Lett. from Palestine, p. 238.

(20.) *The very sands with crystal treasures teem.*

Moses predicted to Zebulon, "treasures hid in the sand," Deut. xxxiii. 19, which Dr. Gill thinks may allude to the discovery of glass. The tradition ran, according to Pliny, that the discovery was accidentally made by the crew of a merchant vessel near the river Belus, which is on the boundary line of Zebulon. Layard mentions glass bowls among the antiquities found in the palace of Nimroud, bearing the name of Sargon, and, of course, fabricated about the latter part of the seventh century, B. C. Opaque glass, found in Egypt, exists of the fifteenth century, B. C.—Nin. and Bab., p. 166.

(21.) *Old man! thou art severe!*

A native of the obscure transjordanic village of Thisbe, among the wild mountains of Gilead; probably a child of poverty and inured to hardship, as may be inferred from his coarse garment of camel's hair fastened with a leathern girdle; Elijah is presented abruptly in the sacred history. We know nothing of him except from his own words and actions. He seems to have been one of the Sons of Thunder, like John the Baptist, whose prototype he was, whom Divine Providence occasionally raises up to utter portentous warnings, to breast the tide of corruption, to inaugurate reforms, or at least to stand up as a witness for the truth.

The general conception of Elijah's character is that of a stern and uncompromising prophet of wrath and judgment, with nothing soft or amiable in his nature. And yet his tender solicitude and fervent prayers for the poor son of the widow of Zarephath; his deep humiliation and self-reproaches in the wilderness; his mourning over the apostasy of his nation; and his considerate desire that Elisha should be spared the pain of parting, when he foreknew that he was about to leave the world; all indicate a heart, so far from being devoid of human sympathies, capable of the most generous, profound, and even delicate feeling.

In these respects, a similarity may be traced between the Tishbite, and the Reformer of Scotland. In each we see the same dauntless and fiery daring, confronting the throne and uttering truths unpalatable to royal ears, at the hazard of being stigmatized as bigoted and fanatical. And in each we also detect a hidden vein of tenderness running deep below the surface, and by those who scan only the surface, quite unsuspected. Knox, when charged by Queen Mary with harshness, protested that, on the contrary, it irked him to appear severe, and that he could not chastise even his own children without tears.

(22.) *If thou*
Must prophesy of ill, to Judah turn.

See the actual prototype of this advice given to Amos. Amos vii. 12, 13.

(23.) *With rights of conscience I ne'er interfere.*

"The principle of liberty of worship, though stated in general terms, refers especially to liberty of *conscience*. The State has no right to ask account of *personal* faith. But when, leaving these private individual prayers and devotions, citizens meet together to worship *openly*, the French government, regarding the important interests of society, has never hesitated to give the State the right of previous authority."—Report of M. Rouland, Minister of Public Instruction and of Worship to the Emperor of France, 1859. (See N. Y. Obs., May 26, 1859.) One might be tempted to think that King Ahab had borrowed his sentiments from the French Minister, so striking a similarity is there in both the thought and the expression; it becomes, therefore, necessary to state that the lines in the drama were written several years before the appearance of M. Rouland's Report.

(24.) *Dread Lord of Heav'n, sole source of day!*

Selden, in his learned work, " *De Diis Syris,*" has exhausted the subject of Syrian mythology. His treatise is the Thesaurus from which all subsequent writers have drawn.

Having shown that "Syrian" and "Assyrian" were words used indiscriminately in the LXX., and that Virgil called Tyrian purple the Assyrian dye (Georg. iii.), he draws attention to the fact, that the Syrian deities were known by Hebrew, not Aramæan or Babylonian names; as Gad, Baal, Baalim, Baalzebub, Ashteroth, Succoth Benoth; Dagon from the Hebrew dag, or fish; Moloch and Milcom from melech, a king. The Hebrew, he conceives to have been the mother tongue.—Proleg. p. 22.

Baal, or Bel, and its plural form, Baalim, are of frequent occurrence in the sacred writings, as common to various gods. From the Phœnician Baal the Chaldeans dropped the middle letter, and made Bel. Josephus sometimes says Bel, and sometimes Baal. He is the Belus of the Greeks and Romans. The name, Lord, originally signified the Supreme Creator. Hence the LXX. render *Jehovah* by the corresponding word *Adonai*, or the Lord. So Hosea says, "thou shalt call me *Ishi*, i. e. my husband! and shalt call me no more *Baali*, i. e. my Lord!"—Hos. ii. 16. This was in consequence of the name Baal or lord having become abused and perverted to idolatrous purposes.

As the primitive meaning of the term signified a lord, possessor, master, or owner, it was applied to various objects of which possession was predicable; as the lord of a house, or owner; the lord of a family, or father; the lord of a wife, or husband; the lord of a wing, or a bird; the lord of horns, or a ram; the lord of the tongue, or a talker; and hence, very naturally, was applied to the sun, the lord of light, which was, according to Sanconiathon, called Beelsamaion, or Beelsamen, i. e. the lord of heaven. Cities had the name in composition, as Baalgad, Baal-Zephon, Baal-perazim, Baal-tamar. In the same way, the Carthaginians, who were of Phœnician origin and worshipped Baal or Bel, (as Dido did, "*a Belo soliti,*") used the god's name in composition, as Annibal, Asdrubal, Adherbal. So Daniel was called Belteshazzar, after the Chaldean god. Bel is alluded to by Isaiah and Jeremiah, and the Apocryphal story of Bel and the Dragon is familiar to all.

An altar in the house of the Mattheii beyond the Tiber, bore the inscription, "*Soli Alagabalo Julius Balbillus Aquila.*" Balbillus was a priest of the Sun in the time of Severus. Selden derives the word Gabalus, by a common change of letters, from AGAL-BAAL, the round lord, or lord of the sphere, as Derceto was formed from *Atargate*, and Baisampsa from Beth-shemesh.

As the Sun, Jupiter, Saturn, Baal, Adon, and Moloch are all employed among the ancient writers in inextricable confusion, the conclusion Selden reaches is as follows : "Since Saturn, Jupiter, Cœlus, Uranus are so confused in fable, that neither Phœbus himself could discriminate between them, or recognize himself among them ; and since that numerous crowd of divinities may be reduced by mythologists to the god Apollo or the Sun, we need not hesitate to conclude that from the one Bel or Baal, or Jove (under which names those who first deviated from the worship of the true God adored the Sun), invoked after the ridiculous manner of the ancients, innumerable titles were derived. The more these titles were multiplied, the more honor they thought they paid their deity, till, as error advanced, what were at first only names of superstition came to be regarded as distinct-deities."—Syntagma, I. p. 140.

It is observable, that Elijah, more than once, charged Ahab with having followed *Baalim*. This might mean either the whole host of heaven, or that not content with the Baal of the Zidonians, he worshipped others of the same name. Baal-berith is the presider over covenants, corresponding to the Jupiter-fidius of the Romans ; Baalzebub, the lord or banisher of flies, in allusion to deliverance from a plague of insects, corresponding to Jupiter Apomuios ; Baal-peor, the lord or possessor of shame, corresponding to the Roman Priapus. Jerome thought this latter, or Baal Phegor, was Maachah's idol.

> (25.) *And flower and river still retain*
> *The mem'ry of that mournful stain.*

"There is also another wonder in this country of Byblis, and that is, a certain river runneth out of Mount Libanus into the sea, the name whereof is Adonis. Now this river, every year, is turned into blood, and being so discolored, falleth into the sea ; a considerable part whereof it tinctures of a purple color,

thereby signifying to the Byblians the time when to begin their
mourning. They also further relate, how that at that very time
Adonis, being wounded on Libanus, and his blood running into
the water, changed the color of the river, and giveth the denomination to the current : which things are reported by the vulgar.
But a certain Byblian of credit related to me another cause of
this accident, which was this. The river Adonis (said he) pass-
eth through Mount Libanus, which consists of a very red mould ;
so that strong winds, arising at that time of the year, carry the
earth into the river, and turn it into a reddish color ; which the
Byblian assured me was the true cause of that accident, and not
the blood they talk of."—Dryden's Lucian, vol. I. p. 242-244.
(The translations are by different hands. That of "the Syrian
Goddess" is by Charles Blount.)

(26.) *Tammuz is dead !*

The prophet Ezekiel, directed by divine inspiration, beheld
within a secret apartment of the temple, upon whose walls was
portrayed "every form of creeping things and abominable beasts,
and idols," seventy of the ancients or elders of Israel standing in
the attitude of worship, each holding a burning censer. From
these "chambers of imagery," he was brought to the inner court,
and between the porch and the altar, he discerned five and
twenty men, with their backs to the temple and their faces tow-
ard the east, worshipping the sun. Thence he was conducted
to the north gate of the temple, "and behold, there sat women
weeping for Tammuz."—Ezek. viii. 14.

There are various opinions, says Selden, about Thammuz.
He has been confounded with Mars, with Osiris, with a king of
Egypt, with an Egyptian prophet of that name, slain by Pha-
raoh ; upon whose death all the images from all the ends of the
earth assembled in the Temple of the Sun in Babylon, where,
suspended in the air, he told them their histories, and they wept
and lamented all night, and at daybreak returned to their places.
Hence, says the Rabbi Moses, the custom of mourning for the
prophet on the first day of the month Thammuz. Jerome con-
ceived him to be the same as Adonis, and to have been called
Thammuz from the month of his worship. Whether the god was

denominated from the month, or the month from the god, Selden is at a loss to determine.

Adonis, according to Hesychius, is the same as the Syrian Adon, or lord, which is merely a title, not a name. So also the word Thammuz signifies *concealed*. The fable runs, that Adonis or Thammuz was a beautiful youth beloved by Venus, whose passion he did not return with equal ardor. He being slain by a wild boar, she prevailed with the infernal powers to permit his return to upper air; but Proserpine, having meantime become also enamored of him, the two goddesses agreed that they should enjoy his company in turn, each six months at a time. All which, understood astronomically of the Sun, symbolized the winter and summer solstices. The Egyptian feasts were movable, but those of the Israelites were fixed. Therefore the festival, with them, occurred in the same month, Tammuz, which was at the summer solstice, answering to June and July.—Selden's Syntagma, II. pp. 240–249.

(27.) *While "Baal! Baal! Baal!" is their cry.*

Much of the worship of the heathen was, and is, an exercise of the lungs. It consisted, also, in great part, of those "vain repetitions" condemned by our Lord; "Battology," the Greeks called it, from one Battus, a stutterer. That no title of honor or other mark of respect might be omitted, they spoke syllable by syllable, and often repeated both syllables and words. A young Brahmin in India has been known to be in the habit of repeating in a day, the name of Siva 6,250 times, and that of Ram, 12,500. Zell, in his Handbook of Roman Epigraphy (see N. Y. Obs., vol. XXX. p. 364), gives a fragment of the sacrificial liturgy of the Field Brotherhood, a sacerdotal corporation of Rome. This curious relic amply illustrates the above positions.

> " Help us, ye Lares!
> Help us, ye Lares!
> Help us, ye Lares!
> Suffer no sickness, Mars, to invade the multitude!
> Suffer no sickness, Mars, to invade the multitude!
> Suffer no sickness, Mars, to invade the multitude!
> Be filled, O Mars! leap to the threshold of the god, and stand
>   there, fat wether!

5

Be filled, O Mars! leap to the threshold of the god, and stand
   there, fat wether!
Be filled, O Mars! leap to the threshold of the god, and stand
   there, fat wether!
Ye twin Penates, the whole people has called you to its aid!
Ye twin Penates, the whole people has called you to its aid!
Ye twin Penates, the whole people has called you to its aid!
      Help us, O Mars!
      Help us, O Mars!
      Help us, O Mars!
Triumpe! Triumpe! Triumpe! Triumpe! Triumpe!"

(28.) *Cut with lancets keen.*

This cutting was not from vexation at their disappointment,
but in accordance with the persuasion that their deities delighted
in blood. Not only were human sacrifices occasionally offered,
as to Hercules, Saturn, Moloch, Diana of Tauris, &c.; the priests
were accustomed, with many mad gestures, to wound themselves
with swords. So did the Persian priests in the worship of Mith-
ra (Josephus, Ant. Jud. bk. 8. c. 13. § 5, n.), and so did the worshippers of Bellona. Tertullian says of them, "to this day they
consecrate to Bellona the blood issuing from their slashed
thighs."—Apol. c. ix. p. 826. Which is corroborated by Lac-
tantius, "Sacerdotes non alieno, sed suo cruore sacrificant.
Sectis namque humeris, et utraque manu districtos gladios exse-
rentes, currunt, efferuntur, insaniunt."—Inst. bk. i. c. 21. vol.
I. p. 74. Similar practices obtained in the worship of Isis, as we
learn from Herodotus: "After the ceremonies of sacrifice the
whole assembly, to the amount of many thousands, flagellate
themselves, but in whose honor they do this, I am not at liberty
to disclose. The Carians of Egypt treat themselves at this solemnity with still more severity; for they cut themselves in the
face with swords, and thus distinguish themselves from the Egyptian natives."—Herod. II. c. 61.

At the great feast in the spring, "the whole multitude is
drawn into the temple, where the Galli, and other priests which
I formerly mentioned, perform the orgies, wounding their arms,
and thumping their backs one against another. In the mean
time many play upon music, and beat drums by them, whilst
others bawl out sacred catches, and this is all performed without

the temple. At the same time, the Galli are also made; for as they sound with the pipes, and perform the sacrifices, this fury of mutilating themselves seizeth upon many, and several coming to see the show, have been drawn thereby to do the like."—Dryden's Lucian, vol. I. p. 268.

" In Hierapolis, the young men always consecrate the shavings of their beards, and the children suffer their hair to grow from their very infancy till the time they cut it off in the temple; when, putting it into vessels either of silver or gold, they hang it up in the temple, and so depart, having inscribed every one's name upon the vessel; the same I likewise did myself, when I was very young, so that both my hair and my name are yet remaining in the temple."—Dryden's Lucian, vol. I. p. 271.

" Now there are many priests belonging to this place; whereof some kill the sacrifices, others carry the drink-offerings; others are called fire-bearers, and others waited on the altar; but, in my time, more than three hundred attended on the sacrifice, having all of them on white garments, and a bonnet [πιλον] upon their heads. A new high-priest is chosen among them every year, who only weareth purple, and a golden turban on his head. There is also another company of men consecrated, as pipers, fiddlers, and Galli, or mutilated priests, besides frantic and enthusiastic women."—Dryden's Lucian, vol. I. p. 266.

(29.) *Perchance he sleeps.*

Elijah had a good right to banter the idolaters about the drowsiness of their god, for it was the general belief that the gods yielded to the influence of sleep. For this we have the high authority of Homer; who describes the gods, in common with the crested warriors of earth, "sleeping all night long."— Il. II. 1, 2. Some have said, that the heathen would not enter into the temples at noon for fear of disturbing the siesta of the divinities at that hour. As for their travelling propensities, the same bard represents Jupiter, attended by all the gods, as having gone

"to grace
The feasts of Ethiopiæ's blameless race;
Twelve days the powers indulge the genial rite,
Returning with the twelfth revolving light."—Iliad, bk. i. l. 423.

(30.) *Sons of the Prophets.*

"Some of the scribes seem to have held schools for public instruction; some of which, under the care of Samuel and other prophets, became in time quite illustrious, and were called the schools of the prophets, 1 Sam. xix. 19, et seq.; 2 Kings ii. 3, 5; iv. 38; vi. 1. The disciples in these schools were not children or boys, but young men, who inhabited separate edifices, as is the case in the Persian academies. They were taught music and singing, without doubt writing also, the Mosaic law, and poetry. They were denominated, in reference to their instructors, the *sons* of the prophets, teachers and prophets being sometimes called *fathers.*"—Jahn's Bibl. Archæol., § 86, p. 92.

The earliest intimation of an organized body of prophets is found in 1 Sam. x. 5. His emissaries saw "the company of the prophets prophesying, and Samuel standing as appointed over them." At Naioth then there would seem to have been a college or school of prophets, a house of doctrine, as the Targum calls it, over which Samuel presided. This presidency was not a chance or occasional thing, for he was "appointed" over them. By whom the appointment was made, or when, or how, we have no means of knowing. In the reign of Ahab, Jezebel cut off the prophets of the Lord, and Obadiah hid a hundred of them by fifties in a cave, probably one of the caves of Carmel, and fed them with bread and water.—1 Kings xviii. 4. It is after this massacre we meet with the expression, for the first time, "the sons of the prophets." "A certain man of the sons of the prophets," called, in a following verse, "the prophet," and again, "of the prophets," accosted Ahab.—1 Kings xx. 35. After this we read repeatedly of "the sons of the prophets," at Bethel, at Jericho, at Gilgal, &c. They seem to have lived in houses of their own, secluded from others, for the sons of the prophets once said to Elisha, "the place where we dwell with thee is too strait for us."—2 Kings vi. 1. Whereupon, with Elisha at their head, they went to Jordan and felled timber sufficient to construct a suitable lodging. "These were establishments obviously intended to prepare young men for certain offices analogous to those which are discharged in our day by the different orders of the clergy; maintained in some degree at the public expense [the log-house built by their own hands hardly looks like it; on the contrary, the twenty loaves of barley, and the full ears of corn presented by a man of Baal-shalisha, indicate that they were aided by the voluntary contributions of the people.—2 Kings iv. 42]; and placed under the superintendence of persons who were distinguished for their gravity and high endowments."—Russell's Palestine, p. 89.

JASODA, OR THE SUTTEE.

JASODA, OR THE SUTTEE.

I.

WHERE lordly Ganges rolls his ample flood,
Adored with horrid rites of lust and blood,
A group is standing, by their country's Pride
And Banians' pillared shade o'ercanopied.
Day's glowing axle downward plunges steep,
To cool its fervors in the western deep ;
And distant towers and burnished pagods gleam
In long reflection on th' empurpled stream.
The west is bathed in floods of molten gold,
While rosy tints superior empire hold ;
The rosy tints by russet are o'ercast,
And Night on dusky wing comes flying fast.
Brief twilight ! where the unveiled orb of day
Pours his directest and his hottest ray.

II.

The hour has come, fit hour for deeds, whose birth
Sprang from the fiends, that darkling roam the earth.
A corpse reposes on a low-built pile,
Where Bramins ply their hellish task the while.

5*

With eye unmoved Jasoda stands beside,
Sparkling with gems, and radiant as a bride,
Through grief, or fear, or opiate's potent spell,
To all the passing scene insensible ;
Unless, perchance, her simple, ignorant mind,
Untaught to think, to childish toys confined,
Now first expands beneath a conscious thought,
With gorgeous visions of the future wrought.

III.

By one sharp moment's fiery sacrifice,
Hopes she to lift her loved one to the skies,
And share his joys ; while the Eighth King of Gods
Shall govern those voluptuous abodes ?
To both, for one short pang, 'twill then be giv'n,
To wander, hand in hand, through Indra's Heav'n,[1]
'Mid spacious palaces, whose roofs of gold
Pillars of solid diamond uphold,
While jasper, chrysolite, and sapphire vie
To shame the splendors of the midday sky.
There balmy breezes play through shady bowers,
O'er limpid pools, and ever brilliant flowers,
Whose blushing petals to the sun expand,
And shed delicious odors on the land.
There softly floating symphonies entrance,
While twinkling feet move in the mazy dance ;
And neither Sickness, Sorrow, Pain, nor Care
With knitted brow, is ever heard of there.

IV.

And does the hope to be so sweetly blest,
With exultation heave that youthful breast;
Is't that her busy thoughts are far away,
And, lost in dreams, heed not the fatal day?
Lo! round the silent, passive devotee,
Haste to their close the rites of cruelty.
Bathed in the sacred stream, whose mystic wave
Hath power at once to purify and save,
On her slow steps the throng, admiring, strew
Garlands, and precious dust of crimson hue,
The golden flower of love that incense breathes,
With ruddy lotus twined, in gaudy wreaths.

V.

The mystic O'M receives due homage first,[2]
Soul of the world. From watery Chaos burst,
Beneath its ripening smile, the swelling sphere,
Which held the germs of all things that appear.
Next, Mahadeva's all-absorbing power,
Lord of the trident, and the parting hour;
Vishnu, with triple crown and flaming wheel,
And conch that wakes creation with its peal;
Chrishna, to whom, in winning grace arrayed,
Her softest vows breathes every Hindoo maid;[3]
Inferior gods the rites theurgic share,[4]
Sun, Moon, and Planets, Water, Fire, and Air.

VI.

The Invocation.

"From your far home,
Celestial Devas, throned in radiance bright,
And ye, propitious spheres of living light,
      Come, Spirits, come!

"From shady vale,
Cool grot, or mountain haunt, with torrents gushing,
Or, on hoarse-bellowing blasts from ocean rushing,
      Hail, Spirits, hail!

"Through middle air,
Swift as the ruddy flash that rends the pole,
Its mortal dross by fire refined, the soul
      To Siva bear.

"Yama we dread,'
Who waits severe, far from the cheerful dawn,
Where the tempestuous South's black caverns yawn,
      To judge the dead.

"Dark spells restrain
And mantra chant, his troop for blood athirst,
Who snuff the fumes afar, and pant to burst
      The viewless chain.

"Appear! appear!
Celestial Devas, throned in radiance bright,
And ye, propitious Spheres of Living Light,
      Hear, Spirits, hear!"

VII.

Thrice round the fatal pile, with measured pace,
They lead the victim, ere the last embrace;
Then place her on the wood, the corpse beside,
Her arms with knotted cords securely tied,
The supple bamboo's length they stretch athwart,
And bind the beating to the lifeless heart;
The heaped-up faggots hide her from the sight,
And all is ready for the torch to light.
That torch, a son's untrembling hand must wave,
Her to consume, who life and nurture gave;
That hand how oft her lip had fondly pressed,
Proud of the babe that smiled upon her breast.
Unnatural task! in the same hapless day,
That bids him mourn a father's lifeless clay,
The boy a dying mother's side must leave,
A self-made orphan, sinning if he grieve!

VIII.

Swift at the torch, around the crackling pyre,
Flashes a raging serpent-coil of fire;
Rapid and fierce the curling blazes rise,
And shoot their forkéd tongues, and lick the skies.
Waked by the scorching pain, but waked too late,
To all the dreadful horror of her fate;
Stifled with smoke and putrefaction's steam,
Her quivering flesh crisped by the sheeted flame;

Fain would she snap the reed and flaxen tie,
But reed and flax her feeble strength defy.
Her eyes are all that she has power to move,
Her eyes in vain she turns to heaven above;
Exulting fiends mock with malicious grin,
And blood-smeared Kalee gloats upon the scene

IX.

In vain she calls a son's forbidden aid,
In vain th' unfeeling Bramins that betrayed;
In vain she shrieks; her piercing shrieks are drowned
By barb'rous horns, and cymbals' clashing sound,
With roll of drum, and thundering gong, and shell
Braminical, and tongue of clamorous bell.
While naked Yogees, and the Soodra crowd,
Swell the discordant din with shout so loud,
Some angel, home returning, well might think,
That unawares he trod near Tophet's brink,
And heard the demons, with infuriate yell,
Burst their dark chains, and storm the gates of hell!

X.

Oh bear me, ye impetuous gales that sweep
On wings of storm across the Indian deep,
Past the broad belt, where sickly Sirius shines,
Where plants luxuriate, but where Virtue pines!
There prowls the Plague-fiend, 'mid the general hush
Of night, a nation's budding joys to crush.

Thick hurtling on the air, by his hot breath
Empoisoned, fly the fire-tipt shafts of death;
If but his shadow o'er the waters pass,
They turn into a green and slimy mass;
Men's hearts for fear fail at his bloodshot gaze,
And melt away as wax before the blaze.

XI.

But deadlier than all plagues that hovered o'er
Old Memphis, or the jungles of Jessore,[6]
There sullen Superstition scowls unblest;
A row of sculls adorns her shrivelled breast:
Her hundred hands a hundred scourges shake,
Each scourge a knotted, writhing, hissing snake.
Frowning upon Orissa's dreary coasts,[7]
A fane as gloomy as her faith she boasts;
A sandy Golgotha around it lies,
Strewn with the bleaching bones of centuries;
Ere the last victim festers in decay,
Vultures and jackals battle o'er the prey.

XII.

" Ye linger, slaves!" the Fiend relentless calls,
" The gods are wroth, haste ere their vengeance falls!"
Her scorpions hiss; the hook, the spike, the car,
Tell how omnipotent her orders are;
The smiling babe she tosses to the flood,
Spurns Nature's laws, and writes her own in blood.

XIII.

Speed the blest hour, by ancient seers foreshown,
Truth's happier reign o'er all that burning zone!
By Bentinck ushered, spread the triumph far,[8]
The Golden Age of the Tenth Avatar;[9]
Mercy, instead of Sacrifice, abound,
And Brama fall, like Dagon, to the ground;
A purer faith supplant the impious shrine,
And all be Christ's from Indus to the Line!

NOTES TO JASODA.

(1.) *Through Indra's heaven.*

Indra is king of the inferior heaven, where reside the 330,000,000 lesser gods, and those mortals whose merits elevate them thither. He was preceded by seven dynasties, and will be followed by seven others. His heaven is eight hundred miles in circumference, and forty miles high.' In voluptuousness it rivals the paradise of Mohammed.

(2.) *The mystic O'M.*

The Hindoos are reluctant to pronounce the name of the Supreme Being; and to hear this monosyllable uttered by a stranger fills them with horror. It is compounded of the three letters, A. U. M; denoting the sacred Trimurti, or Hindoo Trinity, Brama, Vishnoo, and Siva. The esoteric doctrine maintains a great eternal essence, the Soul of the Universe; an emanation from which, the goddess Sattee, by the shadow of her eyes on the waters of Chaos, produced three Eggs, from which sprang the Sacred Triad. The Sattee, or Suttee, is intended to commemorate this goddess having burnt herself to avenge a fancied insult. I am indebted to the Rev. W. W. Scudder for a translation of the celebrated Gàyathri, the most sacred of all their forms of prayer. In Tamil it runs thus: " *Om—poor—puver—suver—tatsavethuru—varène—yam—parko—thayvaseya—themake—theyoyona—perasothayàt.*" The translation is as follows: "O'M, earth, sky, heavens! We meditate on that adorable light of the resplendent sun; may it direct our intellects!"

(3.) *Chrishna.*

Chrishna was an incarnation of Vishnoo, in the form of a shepherd. He was beloved by fourteen thousand milkmaids, and multiplied himself into as many shepherds, so that each maid believed herself sole mistress of his affections. The car of Juggernaut, or Jagger-Nath (which means, The Lord of the World), is intended to represent this Hindoo Don Juan taking the milkmaids to ride in his chariot.

(4.) *The rites theurgic.*

Theurgy differed from magic and necromancy in being the invocation of good gods. (See St. Augustine's City of God, bk. c. 9.) *Deva* is the Sanscrit for Deity.

(5.) *Yama we dread.*

Yama, or Yuma, is the Indian Pluto. His tribunal is at the uth Pole.

(6.) *The jungles of Jessore.*

The Asiatic cholera first appeared in 1817, in Jessore. Unusually heavy rains had made the marshes and jungles of the Sunderbunds, along the Delta of the Ganges, one vast sheet of stagnant water.

(7.) *Orissa's dreary coasts.*

In Orissa stands the famous temple of Vishnoo, or Juggernaut. It is built of coarse red granite. The scenery is dreary in the extreme, and Buchanan, in his Researches, tells of quantities of pilgrims' bones, which he saw bleaching, unburied, on the sands of the sea-coast.

(8.) *By Bentinck ushered.*

The Suttee was prohibited by Lord William Bentinck, Governor-General of India, in 1829, not without violent opposition from the Brahmins. The word *Sati*, according to Sir William Jones, signifies *purity;* and is hence appropriated to the highest act of self-devotion.

(9.) *The Tenth Avatar.*

The Tenth Avatar, or Incarnation of Vishnoo the Preserver, is looked for with intense solicitude by the Hindoos. At the expiration of the Iron Age, he will descend from heaven on a white winged horse, armed with a scimetar, and destroy Infidelity. The Golden Age will immediately succeed. It is impossible not to be reminded of John's description in the Apocalypse, xix. 11–16.

MISCELLANEOUS POEMS.

THE TRIUMPH OF DAVID.

1 Samuel xviii. 6, 7.

WHAT mean tnose sounds that break upon the ear,
Like martial music, faint by turns and clear?
'Tis Saul's returning legions, conquest-crowned,
With captive banners trailing on the ground.
But who is he, the youth that leads the host,
His years too tender for so high a trust;
Before him borne a grim and gory head,
Of giant size, upon a giant blade?

Full forty days the champion called to fight,
Full forty days no warrior sought his sight.
In vain the king to tempt with honors tried,
In vain he roused the veteran soldier's pride;
None with the giant challenger could cope,
Or in th' unequal combat safety hope.

Then left the stripling David flock and crook,
His arms a sling and pebbles from the brook.
With scorn the giant looked upon the lad,
And for a jest his near approach he bad.

Ill-timed his mirth! the pebble smote his brain,
And his huge bulk fell thundering on the plain.
Their champion fall'n, the foe began to quail,
And panic-stricken fled from Elah's vale.
Hot the pursuit.   The roads to Gath that led,
Ekron and Ascalon, were choked with dead.
Saul, the young shepherd's prowess to reward,
Made him the captain of his royal guard.
Forth rush the multitude, intent to meet
And with triumphal pomp the brave to greet;
Gay smiles each countenance with pleasure light,
That late was ashy pale with sore affright;
The magistrates th' advancing troops await,
And elders ranged in order by the gate.

They come! the cornets sound their shrill salute,
The cymbals clash, nor are the sackbuts mute;
The sky is rent with long acclaim and loud,
And not a voice is still in all the crowd.
A band of white-robed maidens next advance,
And carol, as they lead the graceful dance.

Sweet is the mellow flute, at twilight still,
And sweet the music of the tinkling rill;
Sweet are the strains from lark or linnet's throat,
That on the liquid noon exulting float;
But sweeter far a maiden's voice than these,
Rich in exuberant, gushing melodies,

From a young happy heart that have their birth,
In very wantonness of innocent mirth.
Such are the notes, so gay, so jubilant,
The while their choral hymn the virgins chant.

I.

See, he comes ! with pipe and tabor
    Greet the hero's safe return !
Shivered is the hostile sabre ;
    Maids and matrons cease to mourn !
Flow'rets strew of beauty peerless,
    Twine we wreaths of glory's leaf,
For the brow of Valor fearless,
    For the conquering Warrior-Chief !
Saul his thousand foes o'erthrew,
David his ten thousands slew.

II.

" I'll pursue and give to slaughter,"
    Cried the vaunting enemy,
" Ambushed by the springs of water,
    None shall 'scape the archer's eye."
Long, from latticed window leaning,
    Shall Philistia's mothers look ;
Of their sons' delay complaining,
    Counting up the spoil they took.
Saul his thousand foes o'erthrew,
David his ten thousands slew.

6

III.

The brave son of Jesse staid not
  'Mid the bleatings of the fold ;
Though in twisted mail arrayed not,
  Shield or helm inlaid with gold.
'Mid the battle's uproar deaf'ning,
  Shone he in the murky fight,
Like the star that leads the evening,
  Flashing splendor on the night.
Saul his thousand foes o'erthrew,
David his ten thousands slew.

IV.

Lord of Hosts ! in dread and danger,
  Patron and Protector thou !
At thy call appears th' Avenger,
  At thy frown th' oppressors bow.
Shattered is the arm gigantic,
  Hushed the tongue of blasphemy ;
Fled the alien army frantic,
  Rings the shout of victory.
Saul his thousand foes o'erthrew,
David his ten thousands slew.

THE TRIUMPH OF MUSIC.

AN ODE.

2 Kings iii. 12—15.

I.

THREE kings before the prophet stood,
And meekly for his counsel sued;
But of the royal suppliants, two,
Full well the holy prophet knew,
Though forced to ask his guiding word,
Despised the prophet and his Lord.

II.

He cared not, in his righteous scorn,
How high their state, how nobly born,
And, silent, would have turned away,
But Judah's king, less vile than they,
Though leagued to humble Moab's pride,
Had ne'er his fathers' God denied,
Nor e'er had bowed at other shrine
Than that his fathers owned divine.
A prince so generous and so true,
The seer was loth should perish too;

Snatched must he be from threat'ning doom,
Nor find in Edom's wilds a tomb.

III.

" Bring me the minstrel !   Let him stand
And touch the harp with skilful hand ! "
And straight his hand the minstrel flings
Gracefully o'er the trembling strings.

IV.

Soft as vernal zephyrs rise,
Fit to soothe and tranquillize,
Mild as moonlight on the main
Floats the clear and silvery strain ;
Like a fountain's languid hum,
Whose murmurs heavily, drowsily come,
As it purls across its pebbly bed,
Beneath the bending willow's shade.

V.

Now in cadence sad and slow,
Plaintively the numbers flow ;
Wandering, wild, and strangely pleasing,
All the springs of passion seizing,
    Like a spirit's thrilling wail,
        Borne upon the fitful blast,
    When the maiden's cheek turns deadly pale,
        And the startled traveller shrinks aghast.

VI.

But livelier soon the measure bounds,
Lighter the flying finger bounds,
   And wakes a lay
   So brisk and gay,
A hermit's lagging blood 'twould quicken;
   Like the spirit-stirring note
   From the trumpet's brazen throat,
   When the brave their lives devote,
And rush where dangers thicken.

VII.

But hark! the minstrel strikes a heavier tone,
The lowest, deepest, gravest chords upon;
Slowly and grandly, how it rolls along,
A full, majestic, swelling tide of song!
So the pent waves, when once the barrier rock
No longer can sustain the mighty shock,
At once, precipitate, down, tremendous pour,
With thundering, sullen, deep, and long-resounding
     roar!

VIII.

Hold, minstrel, hold thy hand! he speaks!
From his long trance the prophet breaks;
Gazing intent, with upward eye,
Dissolved as 'twere in ecstacy.

A heavenly influence inspires ;
He kindles with diviner fires ;
He bids the waiting kings dismiss their fear,
And tells the glorious triumph they shall share.

IX.

Hail ! heavenly art ! whose potent spell
  Can bid tumultuous passion cease ;
The tempest of the soul can quell,
  And whisper peace.
Should mine be e'er those sombre hours,
When passion madly overpowers,
Oh ! for some friendly hand to roll
A flood of music o'er my soul !
  So, soothed to rest, like his of old,
    Shall my rapt spirit rise,
  In holy calm, prepared to hold
    High converse with the skies.

THE EVENING OF LIFE.

"At evening time it shall be light."—Zech. xiv. 7.

Oh ! grant, sweet Heaven, a lingering ray
To cheer me on my lonely way,
    And guide me down the vale !
The evening shades are length'ning still,
The evening dews are falling chill,
    And strength and courage fail.

The early friends I sadly mourn,
Who, one by one, were from me torn,
    As mourns the widowed dove ;
I've none my joys or griefs to share,
I've nothing left to hope or fear,
    I've nothing left to love.

Then grant, sweet Heaven, a lingering ray,
To cheer me on my lonely way,
    And guide me down the vale !
Then let me gently sink to rest
Upon my Saviour's friendly breast,
    Whose love can never fail !

TOO LATE.

Matthew xxii. 1—13.

I.

'Tis a nuptial festival ;
And the grand old palace-hall
Streams with music, streams with light,
Raising rapture to its height.

II.

But without the gate, behold !
Shivering in the night-wind cold,
Cowers a group of wretches, pale,
Lifting up a piteous wail.

III.

Early had they bidden been,
But despised the festal scene ;
Taken up with trivial things,
Merchandise or pleasurings.

IV.

Now they come—but come too late,
Knocking at the palace-gate ;—
Housed are all ; the door is shut ;
And the Warder knows them not.

V.

Bitterly their fault they rue,
Clamorous for admission sue ;
But, though tears should fall like rain,
Ne'er the portal opes again.

VI.

Heaven's the palace, Christ the king,
Life the time of entering ;
Prompt the moment seize, before
Death shall come and shut the door !

6*

THE APOSTLE PAUL AT MALTA.

Oh, who would build upon the changing flood ;
   Or trust the air his footsteps to sustain ;
Or lean on the capricious multitude,
   Than changing flood, than empty air, more vain ?

"A god ! a god !" cries Lystra, "oxen bring,
   Milk-white, with gilded horns and fillets gay !"—
And scarce can Paul restrain the offering,
   Paul—stoned and left for dead another day.

For him Galatia would her ready eyes
   Have pluckéd out ; God's angel not more dear ;
But soon, estranged by error's witcheries,
   To gall her fondness turns, her love to fear.

With generous haste the shipwrecked crew he leads,
   Shivering and numbed, on Melita's wild strand,
Where fagots pour a cheerful blaze, nor heeds
   The viper fastening on his busy hand.

"A murderer, sure!" the Punic people cry,
  "Spared, for more horrid fate, from ocean's brine!"
But when nor harm nor swelling they espy,
  Their fickle fancy owns him as divine.

Brave Paul! no thought of human praise or blame
  Thy well-poised soul from duty could allure;
Onward thy course, come honor or come shame,
  Conscience thy guide, and Christ thy cynosure.

No sea-girt cliff, patient of driving rains,
  And lashed by angry wind and brawling wave,
Tempest and thunder more unmoved sustains,
  While harmless round its base the breakers rave.*

Be thou our model! ours the same high part,
  Ours the same loyal faith to Heaven's loved Lord,
Ours the same eagle eye and lion heart,
  And ours, from Christ's dear hand, the same reward!

* "Ma come alle procelle esposto monte,
    Che percosso dai flutti al mar sovraste,
    Sostien fermo in se stesso i tuoni e l'onte
    Del cielo irato e i venti e l'onde vaste."
          Tasso, Gier. Lib. c. ix. st. 31.

I'LL THINK OF THEE.

"In the night his song shall be with me."—Ps. xlii. 8

Composed during a night of sleeplessness.

While others, O my God! refuse
    To keep in mind thy memory,
How can my grateful heart but choose
    To think of Thee!

Thine eye had pitied me, ere yet
    I saw my hapless misery;
My Father! can I e'er forget
    To think of Thee!

When Nature shall her beauties spread,
    Hill, dale, and brook, and shady tree,
I'll mark the wisdom there displayed,
    And think of Thee.

Should tempests black the sky deform,
    And men and herds to shelter flee,
I'll smile to look beyond the storm,
    And think of Thee.

Should prosperous breezes fill my sail,
   Smooth wafting o'er life's happy sea,
Grateful, O let me never fail
   To think of Thee!

And if to earth my hopes should fall,
   And friends withhold their sympathy,
Then as my portion and my all,
   I'll think of Thee.

By doubts and fears, if, sore distrest,
   Thy charming smile I cannot see,
Still on thy promises I'll rest,
   And think of Thee.

Whene'er th' uneasy couch I press,
   Nor slumber brings relief to me,
Amid those hours of wakefulness
   I'll think of Thee!

And when is hushed my feeble voice,
   And loosed the silver cord shall be,
Then may my parting soul rejoice
   To think of Thee!

SUBMISSION.

I.

CHILD of sorrow, child of clay,
Weeping through life's wintry day,
Meekly fold thy hands, and pray,
And in sweet submission say,
    "Thy will be done!"

II.

Child of sorrow, child of grief,
Art thou sighing for relief?
Oh, bethink thee, life is brief,
Sow in tears, and full thy sheaf
    At harvest home.*

III.

Child of sorrow, child of hope,
Cast away the cowl and rope,
Nor in gloomy cloister grope,
But to God's blest sunshine ope
    Thine eye and heart.

* Ps. xxvi. 6.

IV.

Child of sorrow, child of heaven,
By misfortune roughly driven,
See the cloud of trouble riven,
See the Bow of Promise given,
      Thy fears to soothe!

V.

Child of sorrow, child of prayer,
Bravely climb Grief's narrow stair,
Leading to a purer air,
Widening to a prospect fair,
      The summit gained!*

    * Ezek. xli. 7.

A TRILOGY,

ON THE NATIVITY, THE CRUCIFIXION, AND THE RESURRECTION.

———•••———

I.

𝔄 𝔠𝔥𝔯𝔦𝔰𝔱𝔪𝔞𝔰 𝔅𝔞𝔩𝔩𝔞𝔡,

OF PROVIDENCE AND THE EMPEROR.

THE Emperor sate on his chair of state,
　　And his courtiers stood around;
And with sinful pride was his heart elate,
As he thought of his power and his treasures great,
　　And the world to his footstool bound.

" This Rome," said he, " so rich and grand,
　　· I found it of dingy brick;
But now, beneath my fostering hand,
Long lines of marble palaces stand,
　　And statues that all but speak.

" And where is the king that against my control
 A finger dares to move ?
My empire stretches from pole to pole,
Where the farthest waves of ocean roll,
 And the painted savages rove."

Then flew a sprite, a lying sprite,
 Like that to King Ahab sent,
To tempt him to rush to the fatal fight ;
And of God permitted, this lying sprite
 To the vain old Emperor went.

And the sprite, he perched on the ivory chair,
 Unseen by mortal eye,
And he whispered into the Emperor's ear,
To number the people far and near -
 That owned his sovereignty.

The flattery worked in the monarch's breast,
 And unto his nobles he spake,
" Go, ride ye east, and ride ye west,
And of all that are subject to my behest
 An exact enrolment make."

But little dreamt, when he spake that word,
 Great Cæsar upon his throne,
Little dreamt Cyrenius, as fast he spurred,
Or Jewry, that flocked to be registered,
 It was all for Mary's Son.

Mary, she travels four weary days,
    To be by Joseph's side ;
Joseph the governor's call obeys ;
The governor's will the monarch sways ;
    And the monarch is swayed by pride.

Dear God ! thy hand the whole did frame,
    And touched the secret springs,
To bring the Lord Christ to Bethlehem,
Heir of great David's ancient name,
    And the throne of the Hebrew kings.

Oh ! cease, ye scoffers, your unbelief,
    Nor longer babble of chance ;
For the meanest peasant, the mightiest chief,
The wheeling sparrow, the falling leaf,
    Are the care of Providence.

II.

A Threnody on the Crucifixion.

I.

WOE ! woe !
Oh ! heart of sorrow, overflow,
For Nature's self, or Nature's Lord, expires ! *
In the broad heaven forgetful of his fires,

* See the remarkable exclamation ascribed to Dionysius the Areopagite, in Lardner, vol. VII. p. 124.   He saw the darkness

The sun doth blindly go,
A mourner sad and slow,
And wrapped in grief and horror, shuts his eye,
His light refusing to man's treachery.

II.

Old Mother Earth
Feels the dread shock through all her nerves,
And from her balance swerves,
And trembles like a ship by surges struck ;
Ne'er since her birth,
Not when man's impious hand the fruit did pluck,
So quaked she to her inmost heart,
As if her very frame would all asunder part.

III.

Upon that cross-crowned hill
All is dark, and all is still,
Dark as night, and still as death ;
Fear chains each foot, and holds each breath.
All is hushed, and all is still,
On that low and cross-crowned hill,
Save a faint moan of pain,
And a dull plashing, as of rain,
Dropping, dropping, dropping slow,
Into the crimson pools that stain the ground below.

of the Passion in Egypt, and said, "Either the Deity suffers, or
sympathizes with one who suffers ! "

IV.

Now is the hour
Of Darkness and its Prince.   With bloodshot eye
Through the close air the gathering demons glower,
And boast their horrid triumph nigh.
They feast upon each groan,
Nor dream that cross shall prove a judgment throne,*
Whence they, in shameful flight,
Like baleful birds of night,
Back to their dismal dens shall swift be driven,
Scarred with the thunder of avenging heaven;
While to the curséd tree,
Death, and Death's master, nailéd fast shall be.†

V.

Beyond the grisly band,
Hover the legions of the blest; each hand
Grasping tight his heaven-bathed sword,‡
Waiting impatient for a signal word,

---

* "The judgment, because the Prince of this world is judged."—John xvi. 11.

† "That through death he might destroy him that had the power of death, that is, the devil."—Heb. ii. 14.

‡ "For my sword shall be bathed in heaven."—Isa. xxxiv. 5. "Inebriatus," says Lowth, "drunk with blood."   "In the sight of God," says Prof. Alexander, "the sword, though not yet actually used, was already dripping blood."   But Dr. Gill thinks the allusion may be to the bathing of swords in some sort of liquor, to harden or brighten them, preparatory to use.

To burst upon the caitiff crowd
Like lightning from a summer cloud.
For they have not forgot the fight,
When all those rebel Sons of Night
Down heaven's steep battlements they hurled
Into the nether world.
They look and long, but look and long in vain,
Their eager zeal they must awhile restrain;
No strengthening angel has a mission now,
To wipe the bloody sweat from off that beaded brow.

VI.

Woe! woe!
Oh, heart of sorrow, overflow!
Life's Lord doth die;
Of mysteries the mystery,
Confounding Nature's wonted laws;
A God the sufferer, and man's sins the cause!
To save our hearts grief that none utter may,
Upon the cross he bled;
He gathered all the thorns that strewed our way,
And twined them round His own dear head! *

---

* Tertullian says the crown was made of thorns and nettles,
as a figure of the evils of sin; but the efficacy of the cross has
taken them away, blunting all the stings of death upon the patient head of the divine sufferer: "*In Dominici capitis toleran-
tia obtundens.*"—De Cor. Mil., c. xiv

VII.

By the thorns and by the spear ;
By the death-pang most severe ;
By Thy wound's uncloséd smart ;
By Thine aching, breaking heart ;
By the unknown agonies *
Of Thine awful sacrifice ;
By Thy dying act of grace,
Pardoning the merciless ;
Tremblingly we Thee entreat,
Christ most patient ! Christ most sweet !
For us sinners intercede,
Now, and at our utmost need !
Matchless martyr ! Sorrow's Son !
Bearing burdens not thine own ;
Let our sins all buried be
Deep in Joseph's tomb with thee !

---

* So read the Greek liturgies : " διa των aγνωστων σου παϑη-
ματων." See Barrow on the Creed, s. xxvi. Those unknown
agonies were, beyond all doubt, the sharpest of all.

III.

𝕰𝖕𝖎𝖓𝖎𝖈𝖎𝖔𝖓, 𝖔𝖗 𝕿𝖗𝖎𝖚𝖒𝖕𝖍𝖆𝖑 𝕳𝖞𝖒𝖓 𝖔𝖓 𝖙𝖍𝖊 𝕽𝖊𝖘𝖚𝖗𝖗𝖊𝖈𝖙𝖎𝖔𝖓.*

I.

YE bronzéd veterans of a hundred wars,
Covered with honorable scars !
What mean the pulse's altered beat,
The stony stare, the quick retreat
Of blood that never froze before,
On Caspian or on Rhenic shore?
Is it the morning-star's bright glance,
Reflected back on helm and lance?
Is it the ray of rising sun,
Shimmering on shield and habergeon ?
Is it the lightning, sharp and red,
That fills a warrior's heart with dread?
  More awful, far,
   Than rising sun or morning-star,
Or sudden flash of blinding levin,
That portent from the bursting heaven !

---

* "Epinicion, or Triumphal Hymn," was the name given to the Angels' Song, "Holy, holy, holy! Lord God of Hosts," when sung in the ancient communion service. It was followed by the Allelujah, which, in some churches, was never sung but once a year; that is, at Easter, in honor of the resurrection of our Lord. So in the Liturgy ascribed to St. James, it is called "the triumphal song of the magnificence of thy glory."—Bingham's Chr. Antiq., vol. V. pp. 32, 246.

To match a foe of mortal mould,
  Trenchant blade, and linkéd mail,
  And sinewy arm may eath * avail ;
But where the champion bold,
His steel against Unearthly Might to aim,
That comes with earthquake tread, and eyes of flame ?

II.

Ye haughty demons ! but of late
Insolent with glutted hate,
  What disconcerts you now,
  And gathers tenfold blackness on your brow ?
Ye deemed a signal triumph was achieved,
When the first mother ye deceived,
  And planted in Earth's breast the thorn ;
Ye deemed redemption nippéd in the bud,
When treason sold the sacred blood,
  And crucified the Woman-Born.
  Behold the Hostage free !
As when refreshed with sleep a giant wakes,
Like willow withes his bonds he breaks ;
  Ended is his and our captivity.
His foot is on the usurper's neck,
The infernal gates with terror quake ;
And fastened to his girdle are the keys,
To ope or shut, henceforth, as he alone shall please.

---

* Easily. " The fort is *eath* to enter."—Fairfax's Tasso.

Back to your dens, ye disappointed fiends,
And howl your empty curses to the winds!

III.

Ye angels! in whose looks do meet
Awe, wonder, joy, in union strange and sweet;
Again, again,
Lift up the jocund chant,
With chorus jubilant,
That sounded erst on Ephrath's midnight plain!

" From spheres of highest worth,
From humblest depths of earth,
Glory to God!
From seraphs' fire-tipt tongues,
From infants' lisping songs,
Glory to God!
From loftiest cherubims,
From martyrs' dying hymns,
Glory to God!
Welcome love's happy reign,
Goodwill and peace to men,
Glory to God!
Thrice holy! Lord most high!
All Earth aloud doth cry
Glory to God!"

The Conqueror comes! the morning light reveals
God's foe and man's bound to his chariot-wheels.

7

Celestial cohorts, close your serried files,
And through long streets of stars, with shout and
      trump,*
And banners spread, conduct the solemn pomp;
While rapture every sinless bosom thrills.
On golden hinge expand the pearly gate,
        The poor Estray,
    That once shot madly from its sphere away,
'Mid heaven's high sanctities to reinstate!

IV.

Ye veiléd women! starting at each sound,
Bending your tearful eyes upon the ground,
What mean those early feet, those spices rare?
    Come ye to cull the choicest flowers,
    In morning's fresh and dewy hours,
A fragrant chaplet to prepare?
    All unheeded, all unseen,
      Fountain, flower, and myrtle hedge,
    Alley trim, and boscage green;
      Graver cares your thoughts engage,
    Wondering much who shall unlock
    The secrets of the caverned rock.

---

   * "God is gone up with a shout, the Lord with the sound of
a trumpet!"—Psalm xlvii. 5. This verse may be recommended
to Professor Longfellow, and all other lovers of the hexameter,
as a beautiful and faultless specimen of that measure.

The stone is rolled away ! and from your hearts
A load as heavy as that stone departs ;
For with that stone is rolled away the curse,
That cast a shadow o'er the universe.

    Mercy's message now proclaim
    In the ear of Guilt and Shame ;
    Crushed and bleeding hearts bind up,
    Tenting them with balmy hope.
    Bid the saint no longer dread
    What Christ's touch hath hallowéd ;
    Radiance from the angel's face
    Lingers still around the place.
    Not in dust the members groan,
    When the Head is on a throne ;
    Christ hath risen ! our brother, He !
    Where our Kindred reigns, reign we.*

* "Ubi caro mea regnat, ibi me regnare credo."—Augustine's Meditations.

DIES IRÆ.*

Dies iræ, dies illa
Solvet sæclum in favilla,
Teste David cum Sybilla.

> Day of wrath! that day is hasting,
> All the world in ashes wasting,
> David with the Sybil testing.

Quantus tremor est futurus,
Quando Judex est venturus,
Cuncta stricte discussurus!

> Oh, how great the consternation,
> When the Judge shall take his station,
> For a strict investigation!

---

* A version of "DIES IRÆ" can hardly be classed among Milton's "things unattempted yet in prose or rhyme," since there are extant more than a hundred translations in various languages. Those of Dr. Coles are among the latest and best. Where so many have made the attempt, a new competitor needs no apology. The present version is offered to the attention of *scholars*, as adhering to the literal words of the original, at least as closely as any preceding.

Tuba, mirum spargens sonum
Per sepulchra regionum,
Coget omnes ante thronum.

> Wondrously the trumpet swelling
> Spreads through each sepulchral dwelling,
> All before the throne compelling.

Mors stupebit et natura,
Quum resurget creatura
Judicanti responsura.

> Death and nature it surprises,
> When from dust the creature rises,
> Summoned to the great assizes.

Liber scriptus proferetur,
In quo totum continetur
De quo mundus judicetur.

> Then shall be produced the volume,
> Proofs of guilt in every column,
> For the world's arraignment solemn.

Judex ergo quum sedebit,
Quicquid latet apparebit,
Nil inultum remanebit.

> When the Judge begins th' inspection,
> Nothing hid shall 'scape detection,
> Nothing shall evade correction.

Quod sum miser tunc dicturus,
Quem patronum rogaturus,
Quum vix justus sit securus ?

> Wretchéd, what shall I be saying,
> To what patron then be praying,
> When the just has fears dismaying ?

Rex tremendæ majestatis,
Qui salvandos salvas gratis,
Salve me, fons pietatis !

> King majestic, clothed with terror,
> Of salvation free conferrer,
> Fount of grace, save me from error !

Recordare, Jesu pie,
Quod sum causa tuæ viæ,
Ne me perdas illa die !

> Jesus ! grant me recognition ;
> Me, the object of thy mission,
> That day, doom not to perdition !

Quærens me, sedisti lassus,
Redemisti crucem passus :
Tantus labor non sit cassus !

> Worn and weary me thou soughtest,
> On the cross my ransom boughtest,
> Fruitless leave not all thou wroughtest !

Juste Judex ultionis,
Donum fac remissionis
Ante diem rationis !

    Judge impartial in decision,
    Grant the gift of full remission
    Ere the last account's revision !

Ingemisco tanquam reus,
Culpa rubet vultus meus ;
Supplicanti parce, Deus !

    Groaning like a guilty creature,
    Blushes mantling every feature,
    Spare, O God ! the poor beseecher !

Qui Mariam absolvisti,
Et latronem exaudisti,
Mihi quoque spem dedisti.

    Thou who Mary's guilt hast shriven,
    And hast heard the robber even,
    Hope to me hast also given.

Preces meæ non sunt dignæ,
Sed tu bonus fac benigne
Ne perenni cremer igne !

    Though my prayers deserve thy spurning,
    Of thy love's benignant yearning,
    Snatch me from eternal burning !

Inter oves locum præsta,
Et ab hœdis me sequestra,
Statuens in parte dextra !

      'Mongst the sheep in safety set me,
      From the goats, oh, separate me,
      To thy right hand elevate me !

Confutatis maledictis,
Flammis acribus addictis,
Voca me cum benedictis !

      While the curst, their guilt confesséd,
      To the fiercest flames are chaséd,
      Call me upward with the blesséd !

Oro supplex et acclinis,
Cor contritum quasi cinis ;
Gere curam mei finis !

      Hear my lowly, contrite sighing ;
      See my heart as ashes lying ;
      To the last thy care supplying !

Lachrymosa dies illa,
Qua resurget ex favilla
Judicandus homo reus :
Huic ergo parce, Deus !

      Oh, that day of woe surprising !
      Guilty man from ashes rising,
      For the judgment must prepare him :
      Therefore, God of mercy, spare him !

TO THE DEITY.

A SONNET.

BEING, incomprehensible and dread!
   Long time have men been feeling after Thee,
   And scanned the heavens in vain thy paths to see,
Piercing the clouds that wrapt thine awful head;
In vain the legendary rocks they read,
   Yet scarce spelled out one letter of thy Name.
   Presumptuous we appear, and much to blame,
Curious to pry where seraphs reverent tread.
Thou the great Ocean of Existence art,
   Without a sounding and without a shore;
While we are but a fragmentary part,
   With all the worlds, chance drops of spray—no
      more—
And of thy lightest breath the helpless sport,
   The surface of Immensity driven o'er.

7*

HOPE.

A SONNET.

O Hope ! the Echo of the Future, thou ;
  The Music of a far-off March ; first ray
  Of coming Joy ; the rosy flush and gay
Of dawning Happiness ; bright haze that now
The Star announces, ere its blazing brow
  Athwart the field of vision takes its way ;
  The soft Refraction, which the God of Day
Gives prematurely to the Guebre's vow.
Our Hopes transforméd Recollections are :
  Persons and place and date are changed ; not so
The story's passionate groundwork, love, or war.
  Past joys, past feelings, Fancy's glass will show,
But varied ; as we reproduce some rare
Old play with decorations new and fair.

GENIUS.

A SONNET.

MAJESTIC emblem of the Omnipotent,
  Thyself creative in a lesser sphere;
  Unbounded thy adventurous career,
Profuse thy miracles magnificent!
To gold thy touch the basest element
  Transmutes; to silk converts the leaflet sere;
  Illumined by thy glance, the mists appear
An arch of glory in the firmament.
The arrow flames a meteor from thy hand;
  Yawning barrancas smile like Eden's bowers;
Even error we forget to reprimand,
  Festooned with grace, and veiléd o'er with flowers.
Why linked with vice, thy birth dishonoring,
Shouldst thou thy plumage stain, and stoop thy lofty
      wing?

WHO SHALL BE CROWNED?

A SONNET.

BRING forth the wreath the worthiest to crown;
  But who of mortals shall the worthiest be;
  Who best deserveth immortality—
A name the listening ages shall send down,
Imperishable, unrevoked renown?
  Is it the soldier breathing fierce commands,
  Pride on his brow and gore upon his hands,
Begrimed with smoke from many a burning town?
Is it the scholar, bent, but not with years,
  Wrinkled and lean, from studious vigils pale;
Who in his nearest volume never peers,
  Unknowing what his own heart may reveal?
CROWN thou the man *himself who knows;* nay, more,
Subdues; of prejudice, pride, passion—conqueror.

THE COTTER'S SATURDAY NIGHT.

A SONNET.

I LOVE the Ayrshire ploughman, strong and bright,
　　As his own share that spared the daisy's blush :
　　What peals of merriment tumultuous rush
At thought of Tam and Alloway's wild night,
The drouthy skellum, and his maudlin fright !
　　Pensive the strain, and soft as evening's hush,
　　When Highland Mary bids the tear-drop gush,
Or Nature's praise inspires a mild delight.
Nor less to memory dear the charming scene
　　Of the douce Cotter's modest, happy home ;
The patriarch's lyart locks and reverent mien,
　　The artless anthem, and the sacred tome,
A Household altar, with a glory sheen
　　That seldom gilds the proud cathedral's dome.

EVENTIDE.

"I have always found that the fittest time for myself is the evening, from sun-setting to the twilight. I the rather mention this, because it was the experience of a better and wiser man ; for it is expressly said, ' Isaac went out to meditate in the field at the eventide.' "—BAXTER.

THERE is an hour when he, whose soul is given
To sober contemplation, loves to stroll
With noiseless step along the dusky glade,
And bare his brow to woo the cooling breeze.
The sun trails o'er the ground his level ray,
And slowly sinking, veils his ardent orb
In canopies of purple and of gold ;
A rich pavilion on th' horizon reared,
Where streaming banners float with regal pomp,
In gorgeous crimson, or in amber clear.
But when the brilliant monarch drops from sight,
And the gray clouds, like courtiers out of place,
Disport in flaunting liveries no more,
Then comes the hour, still twilight's solemn hour,
To meditation sacred, and the thoughts
Which, shaking off the world, look up to heaven.

Then, one by one, peep forth the meek-eyed stars,
Showering down radiance from their golden urns,
And sweetly trembling on the lucid waves;
Then queenly Night with quiet hand unlocks
The gorgeous jewel-chamber of the skies,
And binds upon her pure and polished brow
The sparkling splendors of her mystic reign.
There Sirius burns, a diamond unstained,
And red Arcturus flames undimmed by age;
There ruby, amethyst, and topaz vie,
And milder emerald sheds its paly ray.

A calm and hallowed quiet breathes around,
Scarce interrupted by the rustling leaf,
Or city's distant hum, subdued and faint,
Or cricket's chirp, or katydid's shrill pipe,
Or nestling birds, that, twittering on their perch,
Wake the faint echoes of the darkening grove.
Who has not owned the witchery of that hour,
When, sauntering to some cool, delicious haunt
Familiar to his steps—some rustic bridge,
With striding arch so regularly round—
His heart forgets the trivial cares of life,
Th' ignoble, numerous anxieties,
Earth-born, and earthward tending, that subdue
And tame to their dull level the poor drudge!
Forgotten all!—the strife for power and place;
The scowl of Envy; the envenomed sting
Of Calumny; the oppressive hand of Power;

The hollow smile of cold Civility;
The superciliousness of haughty Rank;
The coarse and vulgar jest of upstart Wealth;
All fade from view; as lovers at their tryst
Heed not the bell that tells of wasting time.

His eye, delighted, scans the varied scene,
Or grand, or beautiful; and as the nerve
The image to the sensory conveys,
(Of busy Thought, mysterious seat and throne!)
His heart with conscious happiness dilates.
Not such from Delphian cleft the boisterous airs,
That fiercely shook the bosom they inspired.
As hovereth, on noiseless wing, the bee
To rob the honeysuckle of its dew—
As openeth its cup the flower of eve,
To drink the zephyr's fresh and balmy kiss—
So the wrapt soul, in quiet transport bathed,
Is mellowed into exquisite repose.

Nor could the Sabine more desire the hour
That brought him to his loved Egeria's side,
Than he to whom sweet Nature's face is dear,
Longs for the moment when he can escape
From dust and turmoil, tranquilly to gaze
On soft green mead, the mountain's waving line,
The crag abrupt, or rivulet's foamy plunge;
Nor recks he, though the world may shake the head,
And scorn the musing, visionary man.

Even in boyhood's years, ere yet he knew
What the strange feeling was, he learned to love
Th' unlonely solitude of wood and glen.
His schoolmates might the bounding ball propel,
Upheave the massy quoit with sinewy arm,
Or straining in the leap, surpass the mark;
In petty sports like these he little joyed,
And though he gazed and wondered at the feat,
He burned not with an emulative zeal.
He rather chose to ramble by the brink
Of some cool plashing waterfall, where shade
Of spreading sycamore and poplar tall
To soft repose invited. There he lay,
Outstretched for hours upon the velvet sward,
While murmuring winds and waters, all day long,
Intoned their dreamy music in his ear.
And so he grew to manhood. What the boy
Did love, still loves the man—to seek the shade,
And people solitude with busy thoughts.

Then fancy bids the scenes of former days
Revive again, and walk their stirring round.
Then Athens from her ruins seems to rise,
And shake the dust of ages from her brow,
Such as at Marathon or Salamis
She frowned the Eastern despot into awe.
Again the sunbeams glance on colonnade
And heavy-sculptured frieze, whose marble forms
Start into life, and lead the solemn pomp.

Again the glorious dreamer of the grove,
With honeyed accents wins the wayward youth.

Anon the vision shifts to Salem's towers,
And that sad tomb where once reposed the head
Thorn-crowned, the heart that bled upon the spear.
Like some stout cliff that breasts the surge unmoved,
The Soldan fierce beats back Lord Godfrey's foin;
Or Tancred sore bewails his Pagan maid,
Killed and baptized by his unwitting hand;
Or brave Rinaldo stays Armida's steel,
Her lovely bosom ere th' enchantress wounds,
And two estrangéd hearts are blent in one;
The tenderest scene the hapless bard e'er drew.

Perchance his thoughts a graver vein assume,
Nor weave fantastic troubles from a shade.
Turned from the spell of genius, and the flame
That lights the patriot's path, the poet's lyre,
He meditates upon the state of man, the ills
That crush his hopes when fairest bourgeoning—
Benumb youth's sanguine ardor—turn to gall
The unsuspecting trust of love betrayed.
So the light sail spreads gaily to the breeze,
On the clear bosom of the placid sea,
While summer skies invite to confidence;
But, ere the song has ceased its buoyant strain,
The black cloud hovers, and the roughening breeze

Increases to a gale ; the swelling gale
Becomes a piping blast ; the blast a storm ;
Then stream the sails in ribbons ; fall the masts ;
The foamy billows o'er the bulwarks sweep ;
And disobedient to the helm, the bark
Is dashed upon the breakers.　There she lies,
Another victim of the treacherous deep.

O beauteous Star of Evening ! lucid orb,
Pure and serene, all bathed in tenderness !
Thou mind'st me of that sweeter Star of Hope,
To sin-wrecked souls on Life's tempestuous sea.
That hallowed beam—may it my footsteps guide
Where those of Eastern Sages erst were led !

THE OLD MAN.

Returnless years of youth and pleasance past,
Why have ye spread the wing, and fled so fast;
And left me thus, in blank amaze to stand,
A hopeless wreck on life's deserted strand;
While memory vainly lingers near the shore,
Bridging the roaring seas and time-gulfs o'er?

A thousand recollections pour their tide;
A thousand early dreams before me glide;
A thousand goodly plans, dispersed in smoke;
A thousand healthful vows forgot and broke.
Vanished, the fond conceits that fired my blood,
Ranking me with the laurelled brotherhood;
Vanished, the visions of high-pillared fame,
A nation's worship, and a world-wide name.
The night shuts in; few sands remain to run;
And life's great purpose scarcely is begun.
Errors and frailties rise in long review,
The ill I've done, the good I've failed to do;—
Oh, human nature! still, 'mid my chagrins,
Blushing for follies oftener than for sins.

Could I thy wheels, inexorable Time,
Roll back !—but no ! a laggard in my prime,
Vain all resolves ; to the propitious hour
Unequal once, unequal evermore.

My hollow temples, sprent with wintry snow,
Bear the deep footprint of the tell-tale crow ;
The eye asks aid, the sinewy limb is shrunk ;
The cheek, once plump and ruddy, wan and sunk ;
The young avoid me ; though, methinks I feel
Light as a lapwing, and as gleeful still.

No more can be disguised th' unwelcome truth ;
Ill fits me now the levity of youth :
To graver cares be my whole thoughts inclined,
And loftier objects fill my serious mind.
On Tully's charming page portrayed I see
The art of growing old with dignity ;
While from the wiser Hebrew I may learn
To wreathe immortal hopes around my urn.

AN EPISTLE TO A YOUNG LADY,

WHO ASKED, THROUGH A CORRESPONDENT, A POST-
SCRIPT FROM THE AUTHOR.

" A POSTSCRIPT " did you say ? oh, no !
I could not bear to treat you so,
    I'll send an ample sheet ;
Pleased, if my unpretending strain
Have power awhile to entertain
    So great a favorite.

Full well, I ween, the courtly style,
That flatters only to beguile,
    You'll not expect from me ;
You wish me, and I feel inclined,
To utter all my candid mind,
    In frank sincerity.

'Tis not the charms that court the view,
The rounded form, the brilliant hue,
    That I most highly prize ;
The gay coquette, the forward flirt,
The caustic wit, the pedant pert,
    I heartily despise.

I love intelligence and grace
In every look and tone to trace ;
    A cheerful, sunny smile ;
An unaffected piety ;
A sweet, obliging temper, free
    From envy, spite, and guile.

When youth is past, and beauty flies,
These captivating qualities
    Survive th' inferior wreck ;
Relume the eye with softer fire,
Each feature with fresh charms inspire,
    And Time's rude inroads check.

Be yours, my friend ! each lovely trait,
That, like the fairy's fabled pet,
    Your lips may drop with gems ;
Each word you utter fall in showers
Of pearls, and gold, and fragrant flowers,
    And rings, and diadems !

PRAIRIE SONG.

I.

Away to the Prairie, away, away !
With the first red streak of breaking day ;
While the bees with their hum wake the dogwood
    flowers,
And the mocking-birds trill in the hazel bowers.

II.

Away to the Prairie, away, away !
Where healthful breezes around us play ;
And leave the close air of the city impure,
With its stifling steams from gutter and sewer.

III.

Away to the Prairie, away, away !
Where never hypocrisy learned to stray ;
But where the brave hunter, bold, manly, and true,
Wears his heart on the outside, all open to view.

IV.

Away to the Prairie, away, away!
And leave the false town, meretricious and gay;
Where all the day long, rings the jargon of trade,
And the one sole thought is, how money is made.

V.

Away to the Prairie, away, away!
And the purest instincts of nature obey;
Our wants are few, and we will not complain,
While the deer and the buffalo range the plain.

VI.

Away to the Prairie, away, away!
No grander temple wherein to pray
The sun, moon, and stars are its lamps alone,
And the winds and the waters the psalm intone.

8

LET THE OCEAN HEAVE TO THE TEMPEST'S WING!

I.

Let the ocean heave to the tempest's wing,
   And the foam-crested waves dash high!
Let the winds through the shrouds all shrilly sing,
   And the creaking masts reply!
Dash! dash! ye waves, with your fiercest spite,
   And drown the ship in spray;
I'll pace the deck with wild delight,
   For I love your boisterous play.

II.

I love to hear the thunder roll
   Above the deaf'ning blast;
And the scream of the petrel thrills my soul,
   As she flies like lightning past.
Oh! give me the storm for a funeral dirge,
   To pour its wail over me;
For a winding-sheet the swelling surge,
   For a sepulchre the Sea!

III.

Down, down, a thousand fathoms deep,
   All on my coral bed !
As sweet as in hallowed ground I'll sleep,
   With the marble o'er my head.
The tide may swell, and the winds may rave,
   And the storm in fury roll ;
My body I'll calmly commit to the wave,
   And to Heaven's sweet mercy my soul.

CONTENTMENT.

"I have learned, in whatsoever state I am, therewith to be content.
I know both how to be abased, and I know how to abound."—PHIL. iv.
11, 12.

YES! Blessed Paul! and well thou didst approve,
By self-denying acts, thy fervent love.
By toil, by pain, by persecution tried,
Thy faithful trust in Jesus never died;
Nothing that well-placed confidence could shake,
Content with all things for thy Master's sake.
By thee instructed, I would murmur less,
And learn the secret of true happiness.

THE MISSIONARY'S HYMN.

INSCRIBED IN THE ALBUM OF THE REV. RICHARD ARM-
STRONG, MISSIONARY TO THE SANDWICH ISLANDS.

I.

Jesus, Master ! let me hear thee
   Speak in tones of tender love !
Fain would I be sheltered near thee,
   Never from thee would remove.
Was it not thy blood that bought me,
   And my costly ransom paid ;
Was it not thy hand that brought me,
   Here the Gospel news to spread ?

II.

I would fain the precious story
   To the heathen nations tell ;
Tell them of the Lord of Glory,
   How to love Immanuel.
Grant me, Lord, thy constant guiding,
   Lead me where I ought to go ;
Let thy Spirit's kind abiding
   Teach me all I need to know !

III.

Give me zeal, and faith, and patience;
  Strengthen all my mortal powers;
And, with heavenly consolations,
  Comfort my desponding hours!
Then, when life's last toils are ending,
  Sighs its last my heaving breast,
On the wings of love ascending,
  Take me, Saviour, to thy rest!

COMPENSATIONS.

I.

LET us aye be cheerful,
  Whatsoe'er betide ;
Life is not all tearful,
  There's a sunny side.
Vernal zephyrs banish
  Winter's frosts afar ;
Midnight's spectres vanish
  With the morning star.

II.

Every deep depression,
  With its chills and blights,
Has a compensation
  In the neighboring heights.
Birds of plumage plainest
  Lift the sweetest song ;
Pangs that rack the keenest
  Seldom tarry long.

III.

Oft the richest uses
 Come from humblest things,
As the marsh produces
 Tribes of brilliant wings.
Larks, at heaven's gate singing,
 Nestle in the corn ;
Mountains, proudly springing,
 Were in valleys born.

IV.

Churned from ocean-chamber,
 'Mid the tempest's roar,
See the precious amber
 Thrown upon the shore !
So each stormy trial
 Yields us fruits of good,
Wisdom, self-denial,
 Strength, and fortitude.

V.

Ravens once did cater
 To Elijah's need ;
And a fish for Peter
 Tribute-money paid.
There's a charming story,
 How the widow's cruse,

Blest by prophet hoary,
  Poured an overplus.

VI.

Thorniest afflictions
  Sharper might have been;
Healing benedictions
  Mitigate the pain.
See the Ark rise higher,
  With the swelling flood;
Ever drawing nigher
  To the Mount of God!

VII.

'Tis a sight of beauty,
  When a noble heart
Bravely does its duty,
  Though each fibre smart.
Courage, Faith, and Patience,
  Principles divine,
In the worst vexations,
  Like the rainbow shine.
  8*

THE OLIVE AND THE PINE

Let others praise, in sounding phrase,
    The olive and the vine,
A southern sun's relaxing rays
    Shall be no vaunt of mine.
Give me the mountain capped with snow,
    The crystal lake beneath!
Though keen the breezes o'er them blow,
    There's health in every breath.

Health of the body and the mind,
    Of fibre and of thought;
Each motion free and unconfined,
    With manly vigor fraught.
The active step, the beaming eye,
    The glow upon the cheek,
The ample forehead, pure and high,
    A thoughtful race bespeak.

Simple in manners and in faith,
    Their stalwart tribes I see,
Intrepid champions to the death,
    For truth and liberty.

Then let them praise, in sounding phrase,
    The olive and the vine;
Give me the bracing wind that plays
    Amid the mountain pine!*

* These lines were written in the house of Dr. Malan, in Geneva (March 8, 1857), after a fruitless winter spent in Italy in quest of health. The first feeling of amendment was perceived at the foot of the Alps, and the fact is gratefully, if not gracefully, commemorated in the foregoing verses.

THE PAGE OF LIFE.

FOR AN ALBUM.

THE Page of Life, like this fair sheet,
Lies freshly opened at your feet,
As yet without a blot or blur,
Your maiden heart with shame to stir.
As years their onward course shall speed,
How will Life's motley record read?
What tender memories shall rise,
What various souvenirs meet your eyes!
Heaven grant that no remorseful feeling
Shall spring to light with Time's revealing!
But may the Angel's pen, upon
The closing page, inscribe, " Well done ! "

THE RESOLVE.

Josephine, when very young, was betrothed to the Viscount Beau-
harnais, but her affections had been given to William de K. When she
was about to leave for France, he solicited a private interview, but
though, no doubt, it cost the tender-hearted girl a severe struggle, duty
prevailed, and she denied the request.—MEM. OF JOS., i. 65.

YES! I have loved thee, all too wildly loved thee,
　As love the passionate children of the sun;
And when confiding, gentle, kind, I proved thee,
　Not blood, but lava, through my veins has run.

To see thee, hear thee, silent sit beside thee,
　No higher joys I coveted than these;
The hope is o'er; but wheresoe'er thou hide thee,
　There's none can rob me of these memories.

From dreams of bliss, a glimpse of heaven revealing,
　Now rudely waked, how mournful is my fate!
Truth, duty, honor, every noble feeling,
　Tear me away, and bid us separate.

Yet take with thee one sigh, heart-heaved and tearful,
　One breathing prayer that happier days be thine;
Thy bosom's lord be ever light and cheerful,
　And round thy starlit brow may roses twine!

THE IDEAL IN ART.

When Rome's imperial eagle flapped his wings
O'er conquered continents and vassal kings;
While yet sweet Maro's was the mother-tongue,
And peasants spoke the language Flaccus sung;
Triumphant Art time-honored Arms displaced,
And her own brow with rival laurels graced.
Then were the Arts as Liberal designed,
Or Servile: these, to low-bred slaves confined;
The Liberal, such as Freemen might pursue,
Demanding intellect and leisure too.

A nicer line our moderns draw of late,
As usefulness or grace predominate.
Such as the principles of Taste combine
With skill mechanical, are styled the Fine;
The Useful Arts an humbler aim attain,
Convenience, or necessity, or gain.
'Tis Taste that must the richest charm impart,
The Inspiration and the Soul of Art.

Ere yet a simpler faith those dreams dispelled,
Beautiful fictions ! of the days of eld,
Behold Imagination's subtle power
Peopling each sunny hill and shady bower !
In every fount a Naiad cool disports,
To every sylvan shade a Faun resorts ;
By her loved oak the Dryad keeps her ward,
And on the sea the Nereid is adored.

Nor groundless quite.   The social instincts lead
O'er universal space ourself to spread ;
Transfuse our feelings, morbid or elate,
And Nature echoes but what we dictate.
The landscape *smiles ; threaten* the angry skies ;
Dark *frowns* the rock ; the rustling zephyr *sighs ;*
The *sullen* pool ; the cliff's *commanding* brow ;
The *laughing* waves that play around the prow ;
The *cheerful* spring ;—who ever dreams that he,
In terms like these, is talking poetry ?
'Tis but the social impulse that creates
Friends out of stones, and planets animates ;
In every lucid wave a picture sees,
And hears a legend in each whispering breeze.

If virgin nature, with a borrowed life,
Thus breathes and speaks, with human feeling rife,
Shall plastic Art refuse her chartered skill,
Nor mould the inert masses at her will ?

Shall she not haste, with trembling eagerness
Her warm conceptions, ere they fade, t' express ?
Till, waked to life beneath her glowing hand,
Embodied, the IDEAL forth shall stand ;
And as it meets th' entranced spectator's eyes,
Emotions, to her own responsive, rise.

'Twas thus the anguished chief Timanthes drew,
But half concealed, and hid the face from view ;
'Twas thus the Dying Gladiator lay,
And thought of his young Dacians all at play ;
'Tis thus wild sounds from forest and from field,
To rhythm reduced, the ear fresh pleasure yield ;
The song of birds, the hum of rural life,
The thunder's growl, the elemental strife.
'Tis thus columnar glories proudly grow,
And nature's lines in stubborn marble show.
From clustered shafts light springs the arch on high,
Again the forest-vista charms the eye ;
While spires and pinnacles profusely rise,
And lead devotion upward to the skies ;
Nature beholds her fairest works outdone,
A solemn anthem in perpetual stone !

THE END.

www.ingramcontent.com/pod-product-compliance
Lightning Source LLC
Chambersburg PA
CBHW031111020726
47495CB00007B/2149